PAYBACK

Maggie Black Thriller #3

JACK MCSPORRAN

Series Guide

The main Maggie Black Series consists of full-length novels featuring secret agent Maggie Black.

The Maggie Black Case Files is a prequel series of self-contained missions which Maggie completed prior to the events of the main Maggie Black Series.

Both series can be read before, after, or in conjunction with the other.

Maggie Black Case Files

Book 1: Vendetta

Book 2: The Witness

Book 3: The Defector

Maggie Black Series

Book 1: Kill Order

Book 2: Hit List

Book 3: Payback

In memory of my wee gran, May, who passed during the writing of this novel. Thank you for your love and endless belief in me. I love you and miss you every day. – Jack

Chapter 1

London, Great Britain

12 June

Maggie Black woke to an arm wrapping around her neck.

Her eyes opened and the bright morning sun blinded her. Panic crashed into her drowsy form like an armored truck and surged through her body, her heart almost leaping through her chest wall.

The arm tightened its hold and pulled her closer. Maggie grabbed at her attacker, their muscles large and firm underneath her grip. She wrestled to free herself from the tangle of covers ensnaring her legs as her mind raced to catch up to her instinctual physical response.

It was fight-or-flight time, and Maggie was no runner.

Releasing her hold on the assailant's arm, Maggie reached underneath her pillow for her weapon. Her hand found the cool metal of the Glock 19, a relic from her past she couldn't bring herself to part with. And good thing she hadn't.

"Hey," said her attacker. A deep voice. A man.

Maggie sprung up on the bed with a hard jolt and broke the attacker's hold. Free from his clutches, she spun and launched herself on top of the man, getting her first glimpse of him from down the barrel of her gun.

"I know you're not a morning person, Mags, but shooting me is a little much, don't you think?" Leon grinned and held up his hands in mock surrender.

Maggie's shoulders slumped and she ran her fingers through her long, blond hair. "Shit."

"You okay?" Leon asked, concern replacing the humor in his tone. He relieved her of the Glock with gentle fingers and placed it on the bedside table before pulling her down onto him.

"Another nightmare," Maggie confessed. Leon's bare chest moved up and down in deep, steady breaths, and she focused on matching him as her rattling heart began to relax.

"Thought as much. Sorry if I made it worse. I was trying to wake you from it." Leon wrapped his big arms around her again and she snuggled into his warmth.

"Always trying to save me." Maggie smiled and leaned in for a kiss.

Maggie lived for mornings like these. While the nightmares were no less haunting, they had drastically decreased since Leon became a permanent fixture in her life. Waking up to him each morning had been a dream she'd never allowed herself to dwell on during her time as a secret agent, working for a clandestine government department known simply as the Unit.

A lot had changed since the puppet strings of those ties had been cut, yet Maggie still found herself caught off guard some mornings when she awoke to the love of her life snoring softly beside her.

Leon tucked a strand of hair behind her ear and stared at her with those deep brown eyes that still held the power to make her feel like a teenager. "I think it's fair to say you've saved my arse more times than I have yours."

"Well, it is a rather nice arse. Would be a shame if anything had to happen to it." Maggie kissed him again and melted into his embrace.

Leon released a contented sigh. "I could stay like this forever."

As if in answer, the alarm on his side of the bed came to life with a series of incessant beeps that refused to be ignored. He smacked it into submission with a fist.

"It's almost the weekend," Maggie said, whispering

into his ear. "If you want, we can stay in bed the entire time."

A deep groan escaped Leon's chest and he kissed at her neck, his full lips brushing over the sweet spot that sent shivers down her body. "Deal."

With great reluctance, Maggie forced herself to roll off of her lover and get out of bed. "In the meantime, how does breakfast sound?"

"Like heaven. I'm going to jump in the shower."

Leon padded to the en suite bathroom wearing nothing but a smile, and Maggie bit her lip as she took him in. Muscles etched across his frame as the morning sun bathed his dark skin, illuminating the array of scars that decorated him like badges of honor.

The shower spurted on with a hiss and Maggie made her way to the kitchen. Willow sat by her empty bowl and meowed with impatience. "Good morning to you too," Maggie said to the black cat, and rummaged through the cupboard for a pouch of her food.

Like Leon, the feisty little feline had become another constant in Maggie's life. Once a stray Maggie took pity on and fed any time she came to visit, Willow had made the decision a few months ago to stick around, taking up residence with a defiant glare that dared Maggie to say otherwise.

Within three consecutive nights of Willow sleeping over and making it clear she wasn't going anywhere,

Maggie and Leon had gotten her a bed, far too many toys, and a collar with her name engraved on it.

The latter took more than a few attempts to secure around the feral's neck, but the metal tag winked up at Maggie as she put the cat's breakfast down and received a lick of thanks from Willow's coarse tongue.

Maggie stretched her muscles, stiff from the previous night's escapades with Leon, and turned on the kettle. Nothing a cup of tea wouldn't fix. As the water boiled, she prepared mugs and set about making eggs and bacon for them both before Leon needed to head out to work.

While his new position meant early mornings, it also allowed him to come home every night, which was a big change of pace for them. After spending so many years flying from one place to the next on assigned jobs, and never being in the same time zone for long, their new way of life was as close to normality as they'd ever come.

Maggie let the bacon go crispy the way Leon liked it and flipped the fried eggs. While far from a Michelin chef, she'd picked up a few skills in the kitchen during her hiatus from working life, using knives for very different purposes these days.

"Smells great, babe," Leon said, coming up behind her and hugging her waist.

Maggie leaned into him and inhaled the mint from his shower gel. His chest was bare, shirt still hanging up in case he spilled his breakfast. It wouldn't do for the Unit's chief to arrive at work with blotches of bacon grease staining his tie. Especially not today when he would be around his superior, Director General Grace Helmsley.

Willow purred at Leon as he helped Maggie with the tea, dancing through his legs until he scooped her up and held her like baby. "Hey, my girl," he said, scratching under her chin. Willow was putty in his hands, having taken to him straightaway once he moved in. She lapped up the attention.

Maggie caught herself watching him, imagining a little son or daughter in his arms instead, and gave herself a shake. One step at a time.

While they'd been an official couple now for almost a year, six months of which living together in premarital bliss, they hadn't broached the subject of growing their family beyond a cat. Neither of them was opposed to the idea, especially now that their lives were as stable as they were likely to get. After years of stolen moments, secret trysts, and false starts thanks to the burden of their job, Maggie and Leon had been happy to simply *be*.

It was all so new, each of them navigating the drastic changes in their lives—Leon with his desk job managing the Unit, Maggie having up and left altogether. Neither had quite envisioned what their future would be like together, but now it was a reality, and Maggie reveled in figuring it out, savoring each moment.

The doorbell rang as Maggie plated up the breakfast.

"I've got it," Leon said, cradling Willow in one arm and answering the door with the other.

"Morning. I need you to sign for this," said their usual postman.

Leon obliged and returned with an A4 envelope in hand. "For you."

"Open it for me, will you?" Maggie said, turning off the heat from the stove and fishing out cutlery from the drawer.

Leon thumbed open the envelope and pulled out a piece of thick cream paper from inside. His brows furrowed as he took a seat and read the contents.

Maggie placed his breakfast down before him and sat across from him at their small dining table. "What is it?"

Whatever it was, it wasn't good. She knew her partner well enough to know that face. Shit had hit the fan, and alarm bells clanged in Maggie's head. She clutched onto her mother's locket, which she'd taken to wearing since leaving the Unit.

Leon cleared his throat and met her eyes. "It's a letter."

"I can see that," Maggie said, reaching for it. "Who's it from?"

"Bishop."

Maggie pulled back her hand like the letter had burned her fingers.

"Bishop?"

Brice Bishop was dead. Maggie had been there when the former Unit chief threw himself off the roof of St. Paul's Cathedral. She'd watched him plummet to his death after he let go of her hand to stop her from saving his life and bringing him to justice.

"From Bishop's lawyer," Leon clarified. "She says there was a delay in settling Bishop's estate due to the police's investigation into his finances."

"I bet," Maggie said. Given that Bishop had pimped out his agents as assassins-for-hire without them realizing it before it was too late, the authorities would have had a time of it trying to sort out how much of Brice's money had been earned from his criminal activities versus his government salary. His daughters would be lucky if they saw any inheritance in the end.

"Anyway," Leon continued, "they've just now been able to sort through Brice's will."

Maggie folded her arms, breakfast forgotten. "What does any of that have to do with me?"

Leon held the letter and the remaining contents of the envelope out to her. "He's left you a personal letter and some files."

Maggie shook her head, refusing to even touch it. "I'm not interested. Throw it all away."

"Don't you want to know what it's about?"

"No, actually, I don't." Maggie kicked back her chair and dumped her uneaten eggs into the bin. Her stomach had turned sour. "Bishop died, and anything he had to say to me died with him."

"You don't need to open it right now," Leon said, watching her carefully as she tossed her plate into the sink and paced across to the open-plan living room.

"I'm not going to open it ever. Nothing good came from Brice Bishop and I'm not going to let him weed his way into my life from beyond the grave."

Almost eighteen months had passed since the truth came out about Bishop and his exploits, and ever since, Maggie had fought to rebuild the pieces of her life his actions had almost taken from her. He'd orchestrated a chain of events that led her to leave behind the only life she'd known since she was sixteen, and she had no intention of looking back.

Leon tucked the lawyer's letter in with the other unread materials Bishop had left her. "I get it. You know I do. You don't need to read it if you don't want to. Take some time and think it over."

"There's nothing to think about," Maggie snapped.

Leon got up and blocked her from pacing. He laced his fingers with hers and waited until she met his gaze. "Whatever is in there might bring you some closure."

"I don't need closure. All of that mess is over with. I

just want to move on and forget what he did to me. To all of us."

There was no telling the long-term, lasting damage Bishop had caused so many people. None of the families of those Maggie and her fellow agents had killed would get closure. None of them could be told the truth of what happened to their loved ones. It would expose the Unit and the department's underground activities, something that could never be allowed to happen. It was far too dangerous, both on a personal level for the people working there, and on a much wider scale that would threaten national security.

"Please, Leon," Maggie said, the beginnings of a headache pulsing across her forehead. "Don't push me on this."

Maggie had no idea how many deaths she was responsible for. Didn't want to know how much blood she had on her hands. The crooked and corrupt, she could deal with. In many ways, eliminating those threats saved more lives than the ones she took, but the weight of the innocent victims hung heavy on her shoulders.

Leon held her close and rubbed her back. "It's your decision. I just don't want you to regret not opening it later on."

He knew the number. Knew all of it. Taking over from Bishop had meant Leon was responsible for cleaning up his predecessor's mess. It had taken a long time to separate each and every case the Unit had worked over the years of Bishop's reign, to investigate which ones were legitimate missions and which had been contracted from outside sources.

That also meant her lover knew how many people Maggie had taken out, her number of off-the-books targets being the highest in the Unit since she was Bishop's favorite. He'd admitted as much to her before he died. Bile rose in her throat at the thought of it.

"I know. I just can't go back there," Maggie said. Leon had remained at the Unit to try to fix the wrongs they had all unknowingly carried out, a feat of personal fortitude she admired and respected. But it was too much for her to go back to.

Too much had happened. Too much had changed.

Maggie placed her hand on her lover's face, the bristles of his trimmed beard tickling her palm. "Things have been so amazing this past year, and I want to focus on what's in front of us, not on the past. We both deserve to move on from the mess Bishop created."

"I understand," Leon said, leading her back to the dining table to sit down.

Maggie wrapped her hands around her steaming mug of tea, cold despite the summer heat from outside, and nodded toward the ominous envelope. "Will you throw it away on your way to the office? I don't want it in our home."

"Of course."

"Thank you," Maggie said as Leon tucked the envelope into his laptop bag. "I appreciate it."

"You're right," he replied, brushing his leg against hers. "This is a new chapter for us, and I'm excited to see where it leads."

Maggie smiled, something she'd done a lot of in the last year. "Me too. Now, eat up before your food gets cold."

Leon complied and checked his watch when he finished. "I'd better head out. Sorry I can't make it tonight. I feel like the shittiest boyfriend ever."

"You don't need to apologize," Maggie said, straightening his tie at the door. "It's not like you can ask the prime minister to reschedule a COBRA meeting."

Maggie knew the drill. Leon's promotion came with more responsibility and with that came a slew of unavoidable meetings. Given the alternative of still being an active agent in the field and risking his life each time he left for work, Maggie gladly put up with the late nights at the office and urgent phone calls that needed his immediate attention. It was a small price to pay to ensure he came home safe every night.

"Still, I should be there with you. This is a big deal, and I'm so proud of you."

Warmth spread over Maggie's chest and she leaned in for a long and lingering kiss, having to stand on her tiptoes to reach him. She broke free before she got carried away and murmured into Leon's ear.

"If you feel bad, you can make it up to me this weekend," she said, her intentions clear.

A grin spread over Leon's face. "I think I can do that."

"Consider it a mission, agent."

Lust and promise filled his eyes as his big hands roamed over her. "I'll give it everything I've got."

"You better," Maggie said, stealing a final kiss before stepping back and opening the door. "Hurry up or you'll be late."

"Okay, I'll see you tomorrow."

"Have a good day." Maggie waved him off and laughed to herself. They'd been like teenagers ever since Leon had moved into her apartment on the Thames, reminding her of their days back in training when they were both naive, new recruits in love for the first time.

She hoped they'd stay that way forever.

Willow meowed up at her, and Maggie made a move. It had been nice playing house for so long while she and her best friend Ashton set everything up for their new venture. She may no longer be a part of the Unit, but staying at home and being a housewife had never been a goal of hers.

While she could hardly list her range of skills on a résumé or job application, she intended to put them to good use. It was time for Maggie to get back to work.

Chapter 2

Maggie raced across the rooftop as six men followed behind her.

Sweat beaded on her forehead as the sun spectated the chase from a cloudless sky. Footsteps pounded behind her, and she sped up in response. They weren't going to catch her.

Not today.

Keeping as fast a pace as she dared, Maggie ran along the edge of the roof as cars whizzed by five stories below. With nothing to cushion a landing other than hard tarmac, falling wasn't an option.

Reaching the end of a pristine set of apartments, Maggie scurried up the adjoining wall of the mid-terrace building onto the art gallery next door, transitioning from Grafton Street onto Dover Street.

A flock of fat pigeons squawked at her intrusion.

They burst out in front of her in a flurry of frantic wings and fled into the air, almost causing her to lose her footing. Maggie stumbled through the confusion of feathers and reached the next building with an added sixth floor.

A drainpipe lined the side and Maggie hoisted herself up it with sure hands and feet, scaling the additional story with ease. It wasn't a victory though. Her pursuers were just as able, perhaps more so.

The city of London stretched out beyond from all angles at her vantage point, her reflection mirroring her movements in the windows of the office buildings across the street. She stole a look behind her where the first of the six men had already made it up the drainpipe.

Dodging aerials and satellite dishes, Maggie carried on and leaped down to the next building. A dart of pain shot up her leg at the less-than-elegant landing, the surface uneven beneath her feet. She slid down the sloping roof, scuffing her palms as she steadied herself.

A cry echoed across the rooftops as the figures of the men came into view, dark outlines against the sun. They were enjoying themselves.

Setting her jaw, Maggie focused and made it to the other side of the building to a series of five identical residential rooftops, wider and more even that those before. Risking a sprint, Maggie tried to widen the gap between her and her pursuers, ignoring the stitch forming in her side and the protest of her burning lungs.

They spread out among the rows of solar paneling

Maggie weaved through and came at her from all sides. Maggie came to the edge and dug her heels to a halt, stopping mere inches from a two-story fall. After a twenty-foot drop, the final two buildings of the long terrace connected to the adjacent Stafford Street and continued on to create a block around the Mayfair neighborhood.

"We've got you," said the leader of the pack as the gang approached. They slowed down, their breathing as labored as Maggie's.

Maggie hovered at the edge, refusing to admit defeat. She wasn't going to just hand herself over. Before she could think better of it, she jumped.

One of her chasers let out a gasp as she launched herself into the air. Maggie sprung, gaining as much height as she could, and reached out as gravity took hold.

Ten feet down, her hands caught the edge of a chimney, her fingertips bearing her weight until she pressed her feet against the brick and jumped again, falling the remaining ten feet onto the lower rooftops.

The leader yelled above her and the others scattered, searching for an alternate route to reach her, but it was no use.

Maggie shot a grin at the leader who lowered his hoodie to reveal a young face and a wide smile.

"You almost had me there," she admitted, hands on her knees as she sucked in air.

"You're mental, you are," Jaxon said, shaking his head. He unzipped his hoodie emblazoned with his parkour team logo and wiped his brow with it, the others finally giving up and coming to join him.

"How did you know you'd make it to the chimney?" Charlie asked, the youngest of the free-running group at sixteen.

Maggie shrugged. "I didn't."

"You really are mental," the boy replied.

"Same time next week?"

"Deal," Jaxon said. "It's Charlie's turn to try to escape next."

"You better practice, then," Maggie said, before she turned on her heels and dashed away.

Once out of sight, she jogged the rest of the way, rounding the block and heading down Albemarle Street until she arrived to No. 27. The Georgian house turned office building sat nestled between a high-end jewelry store and a posh restaurant that served overpriced salads and cocktails to the passing patrons of the surrounding designer boutiques.

Directly across the street stood the impressive Royal Institution of Great Britain, with its towering stone pillars and rows of large windows. While some of the best scientists in the world worked, studied, and carried out experiments for an array of important projects, Maggie and Ashton would be carrying out research of a very different kind from their neighbors.

Taking a final look at the stretch of London before her, Maggie kneeled at the rooftop edge and shimmied

down to the third floor of their new workplace. A small balcony gave her just enough room to stand in, where twin glass doors sat open to welcome her inside.

"You know, most people get their workouts done at the gym."

Ashton Price sat with his feet up on his new desk, sipping an espresso that filled the room with the rich aroma of roasted coffee beans. He shook his head, taking in her sweaty gym clothes, covered with patches of dirt and grime that made her look like she'd been rummaging in a landfill all morning.

"Where's the fun in that?" Maggie asked, avoiding the new white leather chairs Ashton insisted they import from Italy. She crossed over to her best friend and leaned down to kiss his cheek, swiping his cup in the process.

"Haw, you! I just made that."

"Is this the crema blend you were talking about?" Maggie inhaled the scent from yet another Italian import and tasted it. "Delicious. A lot smoother than the last batch."

While Maggie knew guns better than she did caffeinated drinks, she had inadvertently become something of a coffee snob, thanks to Ashton's influence. He drank the stuff like it was water, which, along with his ADHD, left him with more energy than he knew what to do with.

At least he'd had something to occupy him over the last year. A bored Ashton always resulted in trouble, and this new venture of theirs had been just the thing to keep him on the straight and narrow. As far as she was aware, that is, and she'd learned not to ask too many questions about his exploits scamming members of the criminal underworld from their illegally earned cash.

Ashton swiveled in his chair. "Heard you got a package this morning."

Maggie bristled and downed the rest of the espresso. "Then you would have also heard that said package went straight into the bin."

"The old man might have left you some money," Ashton said, getting up and following her out of his office and into the living room that would now act as their central base.

The scent of drying paint and new leather filled the air as a pair of electricians installed the overhead lighting, both women forced to work around the painter and decorators who carried out some last-minute touch-ups to the light gray walls.

"Blood money, you mean," Maggie replied, keeping her voice low. "I don't want anything from him."

Ashton shrugged and held up two different throw pillows. "He's not going to use it anymore."

"That one," Maggie said, choosing the white ones that matched the sofas sitting around an antique coffee table. A huge television screen hung on the wall next to it, and while ideal for a night of bingeing shows on Netflix, the monitor would be used for pulling up mugshots and CCTV footage. "Do you often have little chats with my boyfriend about me?"

"The big man was worried about you, that's all."

"There's nothing to worry about. I just want to focus on what we've got going on now and forget about Brice Bishop."

"You don't need to tell me twice," Ashton said, refilling his empty cup with a fresh espresso from their new coffee machine.

Maggie crossed the room to the large glass panel they'd had installed in place of the interior wall that divided the two main office areas. The glass was empty right now but come Monday, it would be filled with details from their first case. Photos, newspaper clippings, notes written with wipeable markers, and arrows connecting it all.

While the decorating had been left to the last minute, Maggie and Ashton had spent the last twelve months deep in research mode, creating and curating a list of names. Last year's run-in with Ivan Dalca and his syndicate may have left Maggie with a bullet wound, but it had also sparked an idea. Just like the list of agents he had attained to ultimately leak their names in an attempt to take down the Unit, Maggie now had a hit list of her own.

"Hello, Maggie." Tamira Kapoor stumbled in from down the hall, arms filled with routers, hard drives, and a nest of entwined wires.

"He's not working you too hard, is he?" Maggie asked, eyeing Ashton.

"Are you kidding? I hired an IT company to come in and do all this, but she sacked them."

"They weren't good enough," Tami replied, dumping the pile of supplies on her desk next to the state-of-the-art computers and other associated hardware the tech whiz liked to talk to them about. Most of it went over Maggie's head, but whatever Tami needed to do her job, they made sure to get for her. No matter what lay ahead of them, Maggie was certain Tami's hacking expertise would come in handy.

"They came highly recommended," Ashton said, which likely meant he'd paid them a small fortune too.

"I hacked into their systems within twenty minutes." Tamira shook her head. "Shoddy workmanship. It's better that I do it."

Maggie grinned at the young woman. "We still on for later?"

"Yes, please. I won't be much longer here. Just a few things to wrap up and we'll be all set for Monday."

Tami sat down and muttered to herself as she hit the keys on her keyboard at rapid speed, her colleagues forgotten as she got to work.

Monday. The official opening. A trill of nerves fluttered in Maggie's stomach at the thought of it. It had been a long time coming, and now they were finally doing it. Taking down criminals, but on their own terms, and in their own way. No bureaucracy or bullshit from higher-ups and politicians who thought they knew better than experienced field agents. No half-truths or information being kept from them before risking their lives on a job. No one making the decisions on who to target next or how to deal with a job.

It was all on Maggie and Ashton, and while that meant they held the power, it also meant they'd have no one to blame but themselves if things went wrong.

"By the way," Ashton said, "I wanted to talk to you about staff."

Maggie's muscles tightened, but she forced a smile. "What about staff?"

Ashton looked around the place, empty aside from the contractors who would be done by this afternoon. "Other than Tami, we don't have any."

Maggie averted her gaze and busied herself by straightening a pile of fake brochures with their generic company logo on the cover. Maggie balked at the name Engage Consulting when Ashton suggested it, but he had a good reason behind it. *"No one knows what consultants do, Mags. Not even consultants themselves. The HMRC won't ask too many questions, as long as we keep paying tax and sending them our doctored accounts on time, we won't have much to worry about."*

It would also stop people coming in off the street to hire their supposed services. The Unit had adopted the guise of Inked International, an online stationery supplier, for the very same reasons.

"We can handle it ourselves," Maggie replied, back to the thought of staff.

Ashton snorted. "Not with the number of people you've jotted down on that shit list of yours."

"We can work through them one by one," she retorted, still not meeting his eyes.

"Sure, but we need to keep up with all of them. Track their movements, business ventures, associates. All of that takes time. It'd be easier to have employees who manage their own allocated cases from the list until we're ready to act."

A cool breeze swept in from the open windows, white curtains swooping into the air like eager ghosts. Maggie walked to them and stared down at the street below.

"I don't want to grow too big too fast."

"It's not like we cannae afford it."

Maggie knew that much. Given the obscene amount of money Ashton had managed to swipe from the very people they'd be fighting against, Maggie wasn't too proud to let Ash deal with funding their exploits at Engage. The ludicrous Mayfair rent, their salaries, travel expenses, all of it was covered and paid for by the acquired money, and Ashton had set aside a considerable pot to dip into for the running of their business.

"It's not money I'm worried about," Maggie admitted,

biting at her lip as she watched passersby getting on with their day. Businesswomen in smart suits spoke on their phones as they stomped with intent down the street while hackneys honked at each other as they took unknowing tourists the long route to their destinations. What kind of worries did people like that have? What to say at their next big sales meeting? Of what turn to take to avoid traffic? Which city attractions they would venture off to next?

She doubted any of them would be faced with choices that were quite literally life or death. Decisions she'd need to make for others if she were in charge of employees.

While she had turned down Director General Grace Helmsley's offer of taking over Bishop's role as chief, taking on staff would essentially put her in his position, only under a different roof.

Ashton leaned against the door frame and watched her. "You've been dragging your feet about hiring people for months now. Talk to me."

Maggie sighed. Ashton always saw right through her. She'd been trained to lie and manipulate by the best mentors the Unit had to offer, yet she could never get anything past him.

"Taking on our own agents means trusting people," she admitted, getting to the root of the problem. "Call me cynical, but after everything, I'm not in any hurry to add people into our circle."

"Not everyone is a piece of shit like Brice Bishop, Mags."

"Not just Bishop."

"Ah. Nina."

Maggie nodded.

Ashton led Maggie back into the office and wrapped an arm around her. "We've not heard or seen hide nor hair of that one since the mess with Dalca."

Mess was one way to put it. Thanks to Nina, the Unit had almost collapsed and would have taken down all of its agents, past and present, with it. Ivan Dalca could never have gotten his hands on the Unit's classified files without Nina's help. Handing them over had made her vengeful motives clear. Good agents had died in the process, Maggie almost being one of them.

She ran an absent hand over the spot on her stomach where Ivan had shot her. "She's still out there somewhere."

Maggie had shown mercy to her old friend and colleague when she noticed Nina was pregnant. Doing so had saved the unborn child's life, since there was no way the Unit would have allowed Nina to live after her betrayal. Yet that moment of pity, weakness, stupidity, whatever you wanted to call it, had come back to bite Maggie a few months later.

Nina had been a ghost ever since, despite the promise made in her letter to Maggie that she'd see her soon.

"If she has any sense, she'll be in Timbuktu raising that little one of hers."

Maggie took one of the markers and wrote Nina's name at the top of the glass panel, circling it in red.

"I hope so."

Chapter 3

West Sussex, Great Britain

Maggie dodged the fist aimed straight for her face and raised her hands.

Another blow headed her way and she blocked it, the impact sending a pang through her arm.

The woman wasted no time and was on Maggie again, sending a flurry of attacks her way with a wild rage that burned from deep within. Maggie blocked again, and her opponent's dark brown eyes never lost focus as she circled Maggie like a hungry wolf separated from its pack.

What she lacked in technical skill and grace, she

made up for with a relentless, single-minded intent. Sweat dripped down her brown skin, her long waves of curled hair tied back and away from her young, determined face.

Maggie lashed out with a jab and caught her on the chin, sending her head snapping back. A groan escaped the fighter's lips and her eyes told Maggie she was about to strike before she moved.

Using the tell to her advantage, Maggie stepped to the side and the woman hit nothing but air. She received a punch to the back of her head for the mistake and stumbled forward before rounding back on Maggie.

Kicking this time, Maggie ducked from the roundhouse and swiped her own leg across the floor to pull the girl off her feet. She crashed with a *thump* and smacked the mat in frustration.

"You're letting your temper get the better of you," Maggie called, motioning for her to get back up.

Tami glared at her and stood, leaning on the balls of her feet and distributing her weight like Maggie had taught her. Without a word, Tami made to attack again, repeating the error with her eyes and lunging forward.

Maggie spun and smacked her on the side of the head. "Focus."

"I am!" Tami yelled, face flushed.

Grasping her wrist, Maggie yanked Tami toward her and grappled her into a secure hold, pinning her arms behind her back. "Then show me."

Tami struggled to break away, but Maggie held her tight. Arms rendered useless, Tami resorted to legs and feet. She stamped down, aiming for Maggie's toes, but she anticipated the move and avoided it and the following three attempts.

"Come on." Maggie tightened her grip. "Break free."

"I'm trying." Tami squirmed and thrashed, but she couldn't escape.

"Think. What do you do in this situation?"

Tami tried to trip Maggie up, but her attempts were futile, her angle all wrong. Maggie leaned forward to say something else, to prod at her even more, but Tami threw back her head.

No stranger to the move, Maggie could have avoided it. Instead, she let Tami's attack strike true and took the blow. She loosened her hold on Tami's arms, who wasted no time in breaking free.

"Yes!" Maggie wiped at her nose, but she wasn't bleeding. "That's what I'm talking about. You never give up. You always look for a way out."

Tami held her hands on her hips and panted, gym clothes sticking to her after almost two hours of combat training. "I thought you had me there."

Maggie smiled. "You're getting better."

Tami's face lit up, despite the redness from exertion and Maggie's passing hits. "Thanks."

Students needed a win sometimes; otherwise they were more likely to give up and lose interest. Besides,

Tami had earned it. Her months of hard work were paying off, and Maggie noticed a considerable difference each time they sparred. She suspected that Ashton had taught Tami a few of his tricks to get at her, but she didn't bring it up. Tami needed all the extra lessons she could get, and her eagerness reminded Maggie of herself back in training.

Helping themselves to a drink from the cooler, they sat down on the benches of Ashton's home gym and caught their breath. They'd gotten into a routine, meeting three times a week for months now. Surprising no one, Tami was a fast learner.

"Watch out for that tell of yours. Your eyes move before you do, so it's easy to anticipate when you're going to strike. A few games of poker with Ashton will soon get rid of that little problem."

Tami nodded, drinking in everything Maggie said. The young woman was a sponge for knowledge and most of the time didn't need to be told things more than once. Well, aside from one thing.

"You've got to work on your rage too. It's useful, and you can channel it, but you can't let it steal your focus or get the better of you."

"I know," Tami said, rubbing the back of her neck.

Maggie knew that rage like an old friend. It had been a barrier of her own to overcome, and the hardest habit to break. Yet it could be done, and with more time and effort, Tami could learn to wield it like a weapon as Maggie did.

"Are you still seeing Dr. Buchanan?" Maggie asked, toweling sweat from her face. The lessons had been a good workout for her too, since being out in the field had ground to a halt until things were up and running with Engage Consulting.

"Yeah, Carla's great," Tami said, fidgeting with the cap of her water bottle at the mention of her therapist. "She's really helping me a lot."

Thanks to Ivan Dalca, and those before she had fallen into his syndicate's clutches, Tami had been dragged through hell and back. Family massacred, only for her to be trafficked with the intent of selling her to the highest bidder, who would take what they wanted only to discard her afterward like she was nothing.

Without Tami's help and bravery, Maggie and everyone else involved in the leaked list of agents would have died. She couldn't say no to Tami after the girl mustered the courage to ask Maggie to teach her how to protect herself. How could she deny her, after everything Tamira had endured? After the great personal risks she'd taken to help them find Dalca's men and put a stop to their plans?

"Good. Keep going to your sessions. The more you're able to keep your cool in a fight, the better you'll do. Uncontrolled rage makes you reckless, and that can be deadly."

"Got it."

"And if all else fails, remember what I told you?"

Tami repeated Maggie's words like a daily mantra. "Keep calm and punch them in the throat."

Maggie pulled her in for a hug. "That's my girl."

It'd been hard not to smother Tami with love when Ashton first took her in. Knowing her story and what she'd managed to survive pulled at Maggie's heartstrings, but there was damage there that needed immediate attention. Now, after getting used to them and taking the time she needed to work through everything with Dr. Buchanan, Tami had become like the little sister none of them had, and she was the one person Maggie had no hesitation about bringing into their circle. Trust had to be earned in Maggie's eyes, and Tamira Kapoor had gone above and beyond the line of duty.

"Speaking of deadly," said Tami, a conspiratorial spark behind her eyes that shone with Ashton's bad influence. "Can we go to the range?"

"I don't know, Tami." Combat training was one thing, but guns?

"Please? I've been studying online and I'm pretty certain I know what I'm doing. In theory, of course."

"Theory is all well and good, but nothing prepares you for the real thing. Let's just hope you never need to use any of the skills we're teaching you."

Tamira was an assassin behind the keyboard, and

that's where she'd stay. Safe and away from any more danger.

"So, what you're saying is that a practical lesson would be beneficial to my learning?"

"Maybe next time."

"Teaching me to fight is great, but I can't exactly punch my way out of a situation if I have a gun pointed at me. I don't want to be helpless ever again."

Maggie sighed but caved without too much of a fuss after that. Tami was an adult, and if she didn't talk Maggie into showing her how to handle a gun, she'd just ask Ashton. It had also been a while since she'd fired a gun herself, and she could do with the practice. "Fine, but we can't stay there long. We're under strict orders to be ready at six."

Ashton's gym was better than most of the high-end establishments London had to offer, and his indoor shooting range was no different. Boasting a wide selection of firearms that made Maggie feel like a little kid in Willy Wonka's Chocolate Factory, she kept it simple and selected a Glock 19 like the one she had at home.

As it happened, Tami's research had been sound, and she recited everything from gun safety to how she should hold the weapon before firing. Satisfied Tami wouldn't blow holes in the ceiling—or worse, through their bodies—Maggie led her to one of the two firing ranges and prepared the paper target of a person's head, shoulders, and torso.

"Ready?" she asked, yelling loud enough so Tami could hear through the double layer of earplugs and over-the-head earmuffs. While those wouldn't be available in a real-life situation, Maggie intended to ensure that Tami wouldn't find herself in a position where firing a gun was necessary.

With a single nod, Tami aimed and took her first shot. They stayed there for almost an hour, and despite the want Maggie could see in her, Tami wasn't the best shot. Most rounds failed to land, and any shots she'd landed near the head or chest had been accidental more than anything. Nerves caused her hands to tremble, and the more she beat herself up at missing, the worse she got.

Maggie attempted to help, but Tami was too lost in her head. She made a point of checking her watch, reminding her that Ashton wouldn't be happy if they were late.

"Last one. Make it count."

Tami aimed, taking her time to breathe the way Maggie taught her. "You can do this," she said to herself, shifting her stance and frowning with concentration. She pulled the trigger and the shot went wide, missing the target entirely and zooming into the bullet trap beyond.

"Shit," Tami said, handing the gun over to Maggie and pulling off her ear protection.

Maggie placed a hand on her shoulder. "You can't be great at everything the first time. You'll get there with practice."

"Thanks for being patient with me," Tami said, unable to hide the disappointment on her face.

"Come on," Maggie said. "You and I both deserve a drink."

Chapter 4

Maggie held the knife before her.

She sent the blade slicing through flesh, the edge razor sharp like she was cutting through butter. Blood oozed from where she'd stabbed. It pooled on her plate and mixed in with her dauphinoise potatoes.

Ashton grimaced in the seat beside her. "I don't know how you can eat your meat raw like that."

Maggie took a bite of her fillet, cooked to perfection with a charred sear on the outside. "It's rare, not raw."

"A half-decent vet could get that thing back on its feet again."

"They'd have no chance with yours," Maggie said, jabbing a knife at Ashton's plate. "You've had the poor chef cook the thing to the point of no return. Ruined the flavor. And those veneers of yours will have a hard time tearing through it. It looks tough as old boots."

"This is how my wee mam cooks it, and if it's good enough for her, it's good enough for me." Ashton made a point of chewing with his mouth open and making faces like the overcooked steak was the most delicious thing he'd ever eaten.

Tami, a devout vegetarian, laughed at them from across the table as she tucked into her mushroom bourguignonne.

Given the nature of their new business, the guest list of their launch party came to a total of four, including both company directors. Still, the champagne flowed, and the bubbles had already gotten to Maggie, creating a warm, fuzzy sense of contentment within her as she drank and ate with her friends. She could feel her cheeks flush like they always did when she grew tipsy and topped up all their glasses with the delicious brut rosé that accompanied their meal.

"I agree with Maggie," Gillian chimed in. "My Howard likes his steak well-done, so I always make sure it's nice and pink in the middle."

"And how is Howard?" Maggie asked. It'd been awhile since she'd caught up with the forger, but she had taken an instant liking to Gillian when they first met. Maggie had been desperate at the time, and Ashton took her to Gillian, whom he'd hired on numerous occasions for his nefarious affairs.

Gillian made a face at the mention of her husband. "Oh, I don't keep up with what he's doing. Something boring, no doubt. I'm far too busy with work and the kids to waste time wondering about his life."

Tami met Maggie's eyes and they held back a bout of laughter. Gillian didn't seem to mind, though, as she continued eating like they were discussing the weather instead of her complete lack of interest in her husband.

She had on a pink cardigan over a nice white blouse that wouldn't look out of place at a small-town, parent-teacher association meeting. Paired with her bob of mouse-brown hair, a plump figure that she wore well, and her kind face, Gillian had a better disguise than any of Maggie's aliases.

"Is he still seeing the receptionist?" Ashton asked.

"He got rid of her," Gillian said, with all the nonchalance of a disinterested teenager. "Though he's definitely banging the replacement."

Tami placed her hand over Gillian's. "I'm sorry."

Gillian snorted, tossing back more champagne. "What for? I'm loving it. She calls him round on the weekends and everything. He's barely home."

Tami pursed her lips, clearly flustered with how to react, but Maggie and Ashton were used to Gillian's antics by now.

Maggie suspected Howard was more of a cover for Gillian's business than a husband. No one would suspect the unassuming housewife of a generic office manager from the suburbs to be one of the best forgers in the country. Maggie had a few identities of Gill's making, and they were flawless, even by the Unit's standards, and their documentation came from the official offices.

Hired waiters came in once everyone was finished with their main course and replaced their empty dishes with a mouthwatering raspberry soufflé. The delectable dessert was a fluffy cloud that dissolved in Maggie's mouth with a warm, gooey center bursting with flavor.

"You're spoiling us tonight, Ash," Maggie said, taking her time to make each mouthful last.

Ashton winked. "You ladies are worth it."

"Charmer," drawled Gillian, enjoying every minute.

They sat in Ashton's grand dining room, which he only used at Christmas and on special occasions. While he had many homes scattered across the world, his West Sussex estate served as his main residence when he wasn't off in some other country getting into trouble.

Like everything in Ashton's life, he'd spared no expense. His showroom-level décor made the most of the high ceilings and natural light that entered in from large, restored windows of the grand, three-story building.

The summer sun had begun to set in a burst of burnt orange and pinks, casting a radiant glow over the multiple outbuildings, tennis court, and extensive gardens that stretched over the twenty-two-acre property. Maggie ran a finger around the rim of her glass while she stared out at it, lost in thought while the others chatted.

"Gill," she said, interrupting them, "how would you feel about coming to work with us?"

"You mean, going legit like this one?" she said, pointing a thumb at Ashton.

Maggie laughed. "I don't know so much about 'going legit.' We're effectively a rogue organization of highly trained and deadly vigilantes."

"We're the vigilantes who care, though," Tami assured.

Gillian sat back in the dining-room chair and thought it over. "My services don't come cheap."

"I'm well aware of that," Ashton said, finishing off the remnants of the champagne. "I'm sure we can come to a suitable arrangement."

Gillian paused for a moment, then asked, "Would I have to wear a name tag?"

"Of course not," Maggie said, taken aback. They weren't some call center or supermarket.

Gillian's shoulders slumped. "Oh."

"You can if you want to," Ashton quickly interjected, eyeing Maggie to play along.

"And I'd need to travel into London every day, yes? Late nights too?"

Maggie forced back a giggle at the excitement in Gillian's voice. She'd be the only person in all of London to be happy about the commute and long hours.

"Yes, absolutely," Maggie said, not missing a beat.

Gillian appeared to toy with the idea. She didn't need the money, Maggie knew. If anything, she'd likely lose money with her time being taken from building new identities and forging passports and other documents for those in need of them. It occurred to Maggie that removing Gillian's availability might even help their plight in taking down those from her list, many of whom likely sought Gillian's services.

"The kids *are* getting older now," Gillian mused while Ashton popped another bottle of bubbly and served them like the finest sommelier in the city. "They're more interested in going out with friends than they are spending their nights with me."

Ashton's blue eyes shone with a mischievous glint as he filled Gillian's glass. He leaned down and said in a low, conspiring voice, "Howard might even think *you're* having an affair."

"All right, I'm in," Gillian replied a mere heartbeat later, grinning like the Cheshire Cat.

Maggie held up her glass. "Great. You start Monday."

Gillian clapped her hands with glee, then picked up her glass and clinked it with Maggie's. "Well, cheers to that, then. Boss."

"Cheers," Ashton said, and they toasted their new team member.

Ashton placed a hand on Maggie's back when he sat back down. "Nicely done."

Tami cleared her throat before Maggie could admit he had won Gillian over.

"Since we're celebrating, I'd like to say a few words, if that's okay?"

"Of course," Maggie said. "What's on your mind?"

Tami stood and fidgeted with her fingers before she spoke. "A year ago, I believed my life was over. I was lost, and afraid, and certain I would die. After losing my family, I cannot say that I didn't welcome death some days. In a last-ditch attempt to escape from the men who'd taken me, I sent out a plea for help. I did not expect anything to come from it, but you answered my prayers."

Maggie gripped Ashton's hand as she listened, Tami talking directly to her.

"You did what no other could. You defied all odds and you saved me. Saved all the girls like me who had been stolen by those monstrous traffickers. You saved us from a fate worse than death."

Biting her lip, Maggie willed her eyes not to water, but it was no use.

"Even then," Tami continued, "I didn't know what would become of me. I had no family to return home to. Nothing waiting for me in Tehran, other than the threat of being discovered by those who massacred my loved ones. I had nothing, no one, and nowhere to go."

Tami turned her attention to Ashton, who listened without moving.

"Yet, you took me in. You didn't know me, or owe me anything after helping to save me, but still you cared. You've all welcomed me into your lives with open arms, and I can't thank you enough for everything you've done for me. I am forever grateful, and so happy to be working by your side to help people like me out there who have lost hope."

"You saved yourself, Tami," Maggie reminded her. "But thank you for your kind words. I'm glad to call you a friend."

She crossed the room and pulled Tami into a hug, squeezing her tight to say what her emotion-filled chest couldn't get out without crying. A third body joined in, wrapping them both in his long, tattooed arms, followed by Gillian who barreled into them and kissed their cheeks.

"Well," Ashton said, breaking his hold and straightening his royal-blue dinner jacket. "Since we're being all emotional and shit, I've prepared a wee speech as well."

"Oh?" Maggie said, caught by surprise. Ashton wasn't one for speeches or grand displays of emotion.

Ashton dug into his trouser pocket and pulled out a series of note cards.

"Looks like this is going to be a long one," Gillian said, leading them back to their seats.

Ashton waited until they were settled and made a show of arranging his pile of cards.

"Ladies and other ladies. In the wise words of the

great savant and philosophical genius, Billy Connolly, I say to you, 'Life is a waste of time. Time is a waste of life. Get wasted all the time, and you'll have the time of your life.'"

Ashton cheered and tossed the blank note cards over the dining table as he clapped his hands and music played throughout the house.

"Now, come on, let's party!"

None of the ladies needed to hear that twice, and together they moved into Ashton's huge living room and danced the night away.

M aggie laughed as she took a break to catch her breath and watched Gillian try to teach Tami how to break dance. For a woman in her midforties, she moved with more attitude and swag than Maggie could ever hope to achieve.

Ashton scurried off the makeshift dance floor and joined her at the little bar he'd had installed as soon as he bought the place. "Apparently, she used to be in a break-dancing group when she was younger."

Maggie grinned and started to fix a drink for Ashton. "At this point, nothing about our Gillian surprises me."

Ashton sat down and swiveled on the stool across the bar. "You know, when I said we needed staff, I didn't mean pick the first person you came across."

Maggie filled a glass with ice and scanned the gantry for the vodka. "We'll need someone like Gillian to keep up with all the identities and paperwork if we're going to have a team of agents on our hands."

"A team?"

Adding orange juice to the glass to make a screwdriver, Maggie slid the drink over to Ashton and leaned on the bar. "You're right. We need people, good people, to achieve what we're setting out to do. I'd be lying if I said I'm not still apprehensive, but I'm going to have to get over it and start trusting others. Engage needs agents, so let's begin our recruitment search on Monday."

Ashton stuck his hand out for a fist bump. "That's the spirit, Mags. I knew you'd come around. Now come on, Gillian might be a brilliant break-dancer, but I bet she doesn't know the slosh."

"You go on, I'll be there in a minute."

"Off to call lover boy?" Ashton teased.

"No," Maggie lied, and stepped around the bar and into the hall for some quiet.

Leon answered after a few rings.

"Sorry, did I wake you?" Maggie asked, having lost track of time.

"No, I was still awake," he assured. "How's the party?"

Even across the phone, his deep, rumbling voice sent tingles through her. "Good, thanks. Ashton has us all well and truly drunk."

"I'd be worried if he hadn't," Leon said, then his voice sobered. "I wish I could have been there."

Maggie slipped off her heels and padded across the cool tile floor of the foyer, leaning into the phone at her ear. "Me too. But we have all weekend in front of us."

"Sounds like heaven to me." Leon moaned, and she could hear him turning in their bed.

As much fun as she was having, a part of her wished she was curled up next to him, putting her cold feet against him to warm up. He was always warm.

"How did the COBRA meeting go?"

Leon sighed. "This new Tory PM doesn't have a clue about counterintelligence or what we do. It's like talking to a spoiled toddler most of the time. Grace is at the end of her tether with him."

"Just nod your head and do what you were going to do anyway. He'll thank you for it later when his country is free from any imminent threat." She didn't envy Leon for that part of his job. Politicians were the worst, and Maggie was glad she would no longer need to wait on their approval before moving on a case.

"Pretty much what I had in mind."

"Good. Now get off to bed. You sound knackered."

"I'll dream of you," Leon said.

Maggie couldn't help but blush, wanting to be next to him more than ever now. "You big softy. What would your agents think?"

"Who cares? I love you, Maggie."

"I love you too. I'll see you tomorrow morning."

"If you're not too hungover."

"I'm not going to lie, that is a possibility at this rate."

Leon laughed. "Good night, babe."

"Good night." Maggie hung up and clutched her phone to her chest before returning to the party.

Chapter 5

London, Great Britain

13 June

With only the slightest hangover the next morning, Maggie returned to the city and arrived at her apartment by ten o'clock. She'd called Leon earlier, but he must have still been sleeping.

Armed with an especially strong coffee, a bag filled with rolls and bacon for her and Leon's breakfast, and the custard donuts he loved from the bakery down the street, she ventured up the elevator to her floor.

Maggie released a contented sigh as she approached her flat. Other than the headache from overdoing it the night before, life was pretty great right now. A business with her best friend, no boss, great though equally hungover friends, and the love of her life to come home to. There was a time Maggie wouldn't have dared to dream her life could be like this. That she could be this happy.

Juggling her things to grab her keys, she discovered the door unlocked. Looked like Leon was awake after all.

She closed the door and dumped all but her coffee onto kitchen counter. Willow sat glaring, like an angry mother who'd been up all night waiting for Maggie to come home.

"Hello, cheeky face," she cooed, reaching to scratch under the feline's chin.

Willow hissed and backed off before jumping from the counter and running away.

"Someone's in a bad mood this morning."

Maggie hunted through the cabinet for some parac-etamol and swallowed them with a gulp of coffee. An empty pizza box sat by the bin, no doubt Leon's dinner from last night. Olives made her gag, but Leon loved them and ordered a double helping on his pizza when she wasn't around.

"Babe," she called, unpacking their breakfast.

Maggie frowned when no answer came. He had to be home, otherwise the door would've been locked. Agent life removed any chance of forgetting to lock up if you were leaving the house.

Willow popped her head around the corner of the hallway and hissed again.

"Hush, or you'll wake your daddy."

Maggie eyed the filled rolls and debated whether to let Leon sleep longer and let the food grow cold or to wake him so he could enjoy it fresh. He must've been tired if he'd fallen back asleep, last night's meeting with the PM likely keeping him awake.

As quietly as she could, she ventured down the hall toward their bedroom. Red rose petals lined her path and Maggie bit her lip. It seemed Leon had other plans this morning than breakfast and doughnuts.

Shrugging out of her jacket, Maggie followed the trail of rose petals to the end of the hallway. The door sat slightly ajar, and Leon had stuck more petals onto the door in the shape of a heart.

Maggie pried the door open and stepped into the dark room, anticipation dancing inside her. The curtains were closed, blocking out the light, with only the flicker of candlelight illuminating their bed where Leon lay waiting.

"Such a romantic," Maggie said, closing the door.

She kicked off her shoes and walked over to the bed, breathing in the strawberry scent of the surrounding candles and taking in the array of rose petals scattered over the sheets.

Leon didn't turn, and Maggie giggled. For all his

planning, he'd fallen asleep waiting on her. Not that she minded waking him now.

Sliding onto the bed, she crawled under the sheets and moved toward him, desperate to touch him.

"Wake up, sleepyhead," she whispered, wrapping her arm around his large frame.

He didn't budge, proving that he really could sleep through anything. They'd once had to spend an evening in Oslo, hiding in a ditch in the freezing cold during a mission, and he still managed to get some shut-eye while Maggie stayed awake and alert the entire time.

"Honey, I'm home."

Still nothing.

Maggie sat up in the bed and reached for his arm, but she stopped midway.

Something coated her hand.

Something slick.

And red.

"Leon?"

Her heart lurched and she grabbed Leon's shoulder, turning him around to face her.

"Leon?"

Maggie peered down at the love of her life and screamed.

Chapter 6

L eon was dead.

His eyes stared up at her. Unblinking. Unmoving.

Maggie cupped her hands to her mouth.

"No."

Blood stained their white sheets and trickled down his chin. Maggie scanned his body, pulling back the sheets, but he had no evident wounds.

"Leon? Leon, wake up."

Maggie gathered him in her arms and tapped his face. This wasn't happening.

"Wake up!" she demanded, shaking him now. Only then did she register how cold he was.

"No. No, no, no, no, no."

Tears slipped down her cheeks as her mind reeled,

incoherent thoughts crashing into each other. It wasn't real. It couldn't be.

"This isn't happening." Maggie's lips trembled as she caressed his beautiful face. "Wake up, Leon."

Her heart rattled in her chest like a caged animal desperate to escape, the tremoring thumps drumming in her ears. Tears blurred her vision and she wailed in agony more painful than any gunshot or knife wound.

Maggie pulled Leon closer and wrapped her arms around him, leaning her head against his. "Don't leave me," she cried. "You can't leave me. Not now."

Not now. Their life together had just started. They had years ahead of them.

"Leon, please. Please wake up."

Maggie checked for a pulse in his neck, but the logical side of her brain she so desperately wanted to ignore knew it was too late. He'd been dead for a while.

Leon. Dead.

A guttural scream erupted and tore from her throat. Still she held him, unable to let go. Pulling him closer, she cradled him in her arms as her entire world shattered like broken glass, into a thousand unfixable pieces.

Not Leon. Not now.

The blood on his face mingled with a white froth from his mouth. Maggie wiped it away with her sleeve, her body seeming to move on its own as she sat in disbelief. The flames from the candles flickered into burning kaleidoscopes through the hot tears streaming down her face and falling onto Leon's chest.

She fumbled for her phone and dialed an ambulance. Her eyes met Leon's opaque stare again and she hung up. Called another number.

"Still suffering?" Ashton asked when he picked up.

Maggie tried to speak, tried to get the words out, but they didn't come.

"Maggie?"

She wailed again, her nose running and mixing with her tears as she broke down.

"Maggie? Are you okay?"

"No," she managed, the shrill pitch alien to her own ears.

"What's wrong? Where are you?"

"I—" Maggie choked on heaving sobs as her chest tightened, like someone had gripped her heart and dug their nails into it. Like the wind had gone out of her and she couldn't breathe.

"Maggie," Ashton said, his voice calm. "Where are you? What's wrong?"

"He's dead," she wheezed, gasping for air, as if the flames from the candles surrounding them had spread into a blazing fire, stealing all the oxygen from the room.

"Who's dead?"

Maggie tipped her head back and cried out. "Leon's dead."

"Stay right there, I'm on my way," Ashton said. "Stay on the phone, you hear me? Maggie?"

The phone slipped through her trembling fingers and she heaved a lungful of air, her mind on overdrive and unable to keep track. Her heart battered her ribs as she tried to focus. As the panic took over.

Her stomach churned and bile rose in her throat. Maggie let go of Leon, hurried off the bed, and ran to the en suite. Hair curtained her face as she vomited into the sink, her gut wrenching as she emptied her stomach.

A pulsing pain throbbed across her forehead and traveled behind her right eye and down the side of her face, the impending migraine making its presence known. With nothing more to throw up, Maggie ran the tap and watched the water wash it away, falling down the drain and into the darkness beyond.

Her entire body shook, legs almost buckling as she clung to the ceramic to stay standing. Stomach acid burned her throat and she washed her mouth out to delay having to go back into the bedroom.

The dream life she'd been living had plummeted six feet under and fell into a nightmare of her worst fear. She heaved again, but there was nothing left to come up.

What had happened? How?

Leon had his annual physical at the Unit last month. The doctor said he was in his prime. The pinnacle of health. No lingering injuries. No allergies or preexisting medical conditions to speak of. No history of seizures or epilepsy. No family history of either. The Unit made sure to have all of their employees' medical records on hand and reviewed them often. He was fine. Better than fine.

And now he was dead.

He sounded good over the phone last night. It didn't make sense.

Maggie glanced down at her bloodstained sleeve.

Someone did this.

A man like Leon didn't just die in his early thirties for no reason.

Returning to the bedroom, Maggie hugged herself and crossed over the carpet of rose petals to the bed again.

Leon lay where she'd left him, in his boxer shorts like he was still sleeping from the night before. He'd never wake up again.

Someone had done this to him. Maggie pulled out the drawer of her bedside cabinet and retrieved her gun. Just because she hadn't noticed anyone when she came in didn't mean no one was there.

Forcing herself to leave Leon, she crept out of the room and completed a sweep of the house. Willow hid under the couch and hissed as Maggie walked past, like the cat thought she was someone else. On edge, as if some unwanted visitor had been here before Maggie came home.

The place was empty, and Maggie spotted nothing

out of place. Still, she held on to her gun as she returned to Leon.

Scanning over his body in a way she never thought she'd have to, she looked for signs of a struggle or fight. Of anything that would explain what had happened to him. The tears hadn't stopped, and a fresh wave of pain surged through her as she gave up her search, finding nothing of note other than the pooled blood from his mouth.

Leon's eyes were bloodshot, and Maggie gently closed them before gathering the bedsheets and covering his body like he'd simply kicked them off in his sleep. Once she had him tucked in, she lay beside him, arms keeping him safe, and held him as a part of her died too.

Grief overcame her in a tidal wave, and she let it consume her. Let it sweep her away into nothingness and prayed she would never break the surface.

Chapter 7

The door slammed and Maggie jolted from the bed with a start, gun at the ready and pointed at the bedroom door.

Had they come back? Had whoever killed Leon come after her too?

"Maggie? Leon?"

Maggie lowered the gun at Ashton's voice and sat in a pitiful mess on the bed.

Ashton ran down the hall, but he stopped and hovered by the door, taking in the room. "Mags?"

She raised her head and met her friend's eyes. "He's dead," she whispered.

Moving his gaze over to Leon's lifeless form, the fear etched across Ashton's features fell as the blood drained from his face. With tentative steps, he went to the other side of the bed and knelt to check Leon's pulse. But they both knew he was gone.

For once, Ashton had nothing to say. His eyes glazed over and he ducked his head, balling his fists as reality sunk in.

Leon was dead.

Ashton's shoulders shook as he tried to hold it together, and a fresh wave of pain barreled into Maggie like an armored truck. Her friend got up and stumbled to her, pulling her to him in a crushing hug.

It only made things worse. Having Ashton there, having him witness Leon like this made it real.

Leon was gone, and he was never coming back. The love of her life had been taken from her.

"I'm so sorry," Ashton cried, holding her close as she bawled into his shoulder, leaning into him for strength she no longer had.

"He's gone, Ash. He's gone."

What would she do without him? Her life, her entire future, only existed with him in it. All her hopes and dreams. Marriage. Kids. A family like she'd never had. Maggie held on to her mother's locket and wept over a future that had been stolen. Ripped away before it had even begun.

"How did this happen?" Ashton asked, not once letting her go, like he knew she'd fall apart completely if he did.

"I don't know," she managed between deep, choking

sobs. "I came home and found him like this." Maggie looked back at Leon again and closed her eyes. "Oh god, he's dead."

She buried herself in Ashton's arms and let it all out. The unending pain that no gauze could cover, that no doctor could heal. Maggie broke in a way that could never be repaired, and no matter how much she cried or how much she wished it was all a horrendous nightmare, nothing she could do would change things.

For all she was capable of, for all she had done as an agent, and all the lives she'd saved, there was nothing she could do to save Leon now.

Maggie didn't know how long they sat there. It could have been five minutes or five hours. Her muscles ached from exertion, throat hoarse from the cries of a pain she'd never known. She'd survived countless injuries before, had hundreds of close encounters that ended in her needing to be fixed up. To have her wounds treated and healed. Yet nothing compared to this. This wound would never heal. It would never stop hurting. She'd been torn open and could never be put back together. There was no coming back from this.

Footsteps filtered in from the living room, the unmistakable cocking of guns pricking Maggie's ears. Instinct more than anything kicked in and she pulled herself from Ashton, grabbing her gun. They wouldn't take Ashton from her. He was all she had left.

"It's okay, I called them," Ashton said, lowering her

gun and turning his attention to the new arrivals. "In the bedroom. The place is clear."

The footsteps grew louder, and people clad in black bulletproof vests and rifles spilled into the room. Director General Grace Helmsley entered behind them, dressed in her usual no-nonsense power suit, the cut of her bob as severe as her cheekbones as she scanned the area with eyes that missed nothing.

Those hard, cunning eyes latched on to Leon's form and for a second, Maggie caught the human behind the mask. Witnessed the sharp inhale of shock as understanding settled into Helmsley.

She wasn't the only one. Familiar faces surrounded Maggie, each of her former colleagues fighting to stay professional as they eyed the dead body of their chief. No one spoke, and the air grew thick with tension.

Grace stepped forward, sentried by two guards who Maggie had had a run-in with before, and she placed a wrinkled hand on Leon's form. "Call it in," she ordered, clearing her throat. She straightened her suit jacket and turned to Maggie and Ashton. "What happened?"

"She came home this morning and found him like this."

Helmsley stared pointedly at the scattered rose petals and arched an eyebrow.

Ashton shrugged, rubbing Maggie's back while the agents around them shuffled on their feet, guns lowered and awaiting orders. Helmsley took a deep, shaking breath before she continued.

"Harris, I want forensics down here, now. Hutchings, get me CCTV footage for the building and the surrounding area. Clifford, you and Hamilton begin questioning the neighbors. Someone must have seen something. The rest of you, I want this place cordoned off. The entire street. No one gets in or out without being searched and questioned. Lock everything down."

Grace nodded her head to the door, and they all exited, her personal bodyguards waiting outside in the hall.

"He's been poisoned," Maggie told her, certain of it. She'd seen enough poisonings to know the signs.

"By whom?" Grace asked, her steely resolve returning as she kicked into work mode.

A surge of anger coursing through Maggie. "You tell me. What was the COBRA meeting about last night?"

Grace pursed her lips. "You know I can't tell you that."

"Who's involved?" Maggie demanded, straightening her back. "What case was Leon working?"

"It's classified."

Before she knew it, Maggie was off the bed, inches away from Helmsley. "Classified? Really?"

"You're no longer an agent, Maggie. You made that choice."

Maggie's hands itched and it took every last ounce of

restraint she had not to smack her old superior. "If you know something, anything, about what happened, you will tell me. One way or another."

Grace's guards moved to the foot of the door and watched Maggie with hands nearing their concealed weapons. Helmsley waved them off and faced Maggie without so much as a flinch.

"I know this is a difficult time for you, but don't you ever threaten me."

Maggie didn't budge, her feet rooted to the ground. "Threats are for people like you. I make promises."

A hand touched her shoulder. "Calm down," Ashton said.

Maggie glared at him, enraged that he would take Grace's side. She knew what case Leon was working. Knew who might have done this to him, yet she refused to tell them. "Someone did this to him!" she yelled.

"I think I know who."

Maggie and Ashton focused on Grace who moved to the dresser at the far side of the room. Candles flickered as she passed, their wicks almost burned to nothing. Rose petals had been placed across the surface and stuck around the large, round mirror in the center.

A message had been written across it in Maggie's red lipstick:

Now you know how it feels.

Nina xoxo

Chapter 8

West Sussex, Great Britain
14 June

"Leon!"

Maggie sat up and sucked in a lungful of air. It took a moment for her mind to catch up, her eyes searching as they settled across the unfamiliar shadows of the room.

Pulling her knees up from under the sheets, Maggie hugged her legs and bit back tears. The bedsheets were overly warm and coated with sweat, her hair a tangled mess that stuck to her face.

Reality crashed in like an unwelcome guest, every

inch of her weak with an emptiness in her chest, as if someone had carved out her heart with a serrated blade.

The temptation to lie back down and let sleep carry her away grew stronger, but her bladder ached, and she forced herself to slide out of bed.

Padding to the bathroom of one of Ashton's guest rooms, she relieved herself, keeping the lights off. Her head pulsed with tension, the only feeling other than the complete sense of overwhelming numbness. She was hollow. Nothing but an empty shell.

Light came in through the bathroom window, illuminating the rise of the sun the blackout curtains hid from her while in bed. A new day. A day without Leon in it.

Nothing awaited Maggie in her sleep but the reliving of the nightmare of her reality. Instead, she yanked off her clothes from the day before, having been too distraught to change into nightclothes, and stepped into the shower. The water hissed to life and Maggie closed her eyes, focusing on the heat and steady pulse of the jet on her back.

After crying until she didn't think she had any tears left, she scrubbed herself clean, dried off, and pulled on some spare clothes someone had laid out for her on the chair by the window.

Maggie opened the curtains and winced at the intensity assaulting her. It was too bright. Too beautiful as it bathed Ashton's estate with warmth and turned the sky a brilliant summer orange. She closed them again and stood in the middle of the room, her mind vacant.

What did she do now?

The stairs creaked as she ventured downstairs, quiet for the birds singing their morning songs outside. The aroma of coffee filled the air, and she entered the kitchen to find Ashton and Tami sitting at the breakfast table in silence.

A clock ticked in the background. Maggie didn't bother checking the time. What did it matter?

An almost-empty bottle of whisky sat next to the cafetière on the table and Ashton poured what was left into his cup of steaming coffee. Tami's sat untouched. Bags hung under their eyes like they hadn't slept, Ashton in the same clothes he'd had on when he rushed to her apartment.

Maggie wasn't sure when they left her place. Forensics had arrived along with the medical examiner, both there to carry out their inspections. Leaving Leon hadn't been pretty, and it took Ashton and three other agents to remove Maggie from the bedroom.

At some point, Ashton drove them back here, but the rest of the day was a blur. She couldn't recall much after being dragged away from Leon. After she'd said her final goodbye.

Ashton and Tami stirred when they spotted her.

"Good morning, Maggie," Tami said in a quiet voice, like Maggie might get spooked and run off.

"Is it?"

Tami got up from her chair and without warning threw her arms around Maggie. It was the last thing she wanted right now, barely holding herself together, but she returned the embrace for the girl's sake. Maggie wasn't the only one who'd lost someone. Tami had loved Leon too, and she brought out his playful side while they exchanged teasing jabs and debated over *Star Wars* theories. If Ashton had been Leon's brother, it hadn't taken Tami long to feel like his little sister.

"I can't believe it," she said in Maggie's ear. "I don't know what to say."

Maggie pulled back and tucked a strand of Tami's hair behind her ear. "I don't either."

Ashton gave her a silent nod, seeming to sense her mood. He poured half his laced coffee into an empty cup and slid it across the table before an empty seat.

Maggie sat and wrapped her hands around the mug. They stayed like that for a while, none of them talking as the morning passed by.

A thought struck Maggie so hard, she almost fell over. How could she forget? "Oh god, Sade and Idris. Do they know yet? I should have—"

Maggie pushed back her chair to leave, but Ashton took her hand and motioned for her to sit back down.

"Grace went after they'd finished at your flat."

"Are they okay?" Maggie bowed her head and held up a hand to stop Ashton from answering. Of course, they weren't okay. Their pride and joy, their only child, had been murdered. Leon had meant so much to them all, had touched all their lives for the better.

"What did Grace tell them?" she asked.

As far as Leon's parents were concerned, he was a senior manager at a stationery company. All agents were under strict orders not to reveal their jobs or affiliation to anyone. Keeping your loved ones in the dark was mandatory, but it protected them too. The less they knew about any of it, the better. Until something like this happened.

When someone from the Unit died, most of the time, the families were given some fabrication about how their loved one had perished. She could only imagine what tale Grace would create to tell Sade and Idris.

Everyone would be in on it, even the medical examiner. Whatever would go on Leon's death certificate, the cause of death would not be listed as poisoning. A road accident or the like would be the best cover. Something common that would also stop the family from being able to view the body.

The body.

Maggie shivered.

They grew quiet again, each lost in their thoughts and grief. Maggie was a total loss on what to say. A little bell chimed, and Willow sauntered in from outside in the garden, slipping through the opened window. The cat made a direct line for Maggie and jumped into her lap, meowing and rubbing her furry head against her.

"I didn't want to leave her behind," Ashton said. "Too many strangers going in and out. It would have stressed her out."

"Right," Maggie said, running her hand along Willow's back.

A few more long minutes ticked past, each second taking her further and further away from the last time she touched Leon. The last time she'd spoken with him. The last time she told him she loved him. Maggie looked between Tami and Ashton, her bottom lip quivering.

"What am I going to do?"

And just when she didn't think she had any more tears left, Maggie broke down and cried in the arms of her friends.

———

A cool night breeze swept by as Maggie walked alone through Ashton's garden. Her eyes nipped, swollen and red. The full moon glowed above as she traversed, needing some time away from Ashton and Tami who were doing everything they could to be attentive to her needs.

Even though they meant well, it suffocated her.

Crickets chirped among the grass and the bright flowers in full bloom. The heat from the day had lingered long after the sun departed, yet she wrapped Ashton's oversized jacket around her shoulders while she wandered.

Maggie opened the oval locket that hung from the silver chain around her neck and rubbed her thumb over the photograph inside. Eyes the same ice blue as her own stared back at her, her mother smiling with a two-year-old Maggie on her lap. Her only family.

Death wasn't new to Maggie. After her mother died in the car crash when Maggie was only six, she recalled feeling like she had no one in the world. For many years afterward, she hadn't. The absence of her mother growing up had been an almost physical pain as she endured a life in the foster system, being passed from pillar to post, from one house to the other with strangers who didn't know her. Who didn't love her.

Maggie closed the locket and continued walking through the garden, not taking in any of its beauty. Too lost in her thoughts.

Death followed her after her mother, but the next time she encountered it, it was by her own hand at sixteen. Killing someone had never been part of her plan, yet even now, Maggie couldn't deny her last foster father had it coming. She'd saved those girls from him, and in a way, she'd saved herself.

When the murder finally caught up with her and she found herself arrested, Maggie believed her life to be over. Looking back, the choice offered by Brice Bishop hadn't been much of a choice at all. Faced with either life in prison for her crimes or going with him to work for the government didn't require much thinking on Maggie's part. While the path she'd gone down had resulted in more death, she discovered love of a different kind from what she'd had with her mother.

Maggie left the garden and wound her way through the courtyard, the trickling of Ashton's Grecian-style water fountain splashing in the background. Instead of heading back inside, she found herself venturing in the opposite direction toward the cluster of outbuildings. She wasn't ready to return yet, to have to sit while Ashton and Tami tiptoed around her. To see her own grief reflected in their stricken faces, or the pity they tried to hide behind their eyes.

Her question to them circled in her mind. What did she do now?

Leon had entered her life at a time when she needed someone the most. It didn't take long for Maggie to grow feelings for him. How could she not? A handsome young man, a year older than she was, who genuinely seemed to care for her. He never judged her or expected anything from her. Being around Leon made her feel safe, like she'd finally found a home. She loved him for that, and a million other things. She loved him from all those years ago, and her feelings had only intensified.

Maggie balled her fists as she passed the gym. She'd been happy. Happier than she ever thought possible. She'd found a love in Leon many only wished for.

Someone to share her life with. To have babies with. To grow old with. She was his and he was hers, and Nina had taken that from her like it was nothing. Like it was some warped game of tit for tat.

Her fingernails dug into her palms as the emptiness inside her began to fill. Not with sorrow, but with a much more familiar feeling. One she welcomed. One that pushed away all others and burned through her like wildfire.

Rage.

Marching to the farthest outbuilding, Maggie pushed the door to the firing range open so hard, the door hit the adjacent wall and the glass rained across the floor in rough-cut diamonds.

Shards cracked and crumbled under her boots as she turned into the armory, her anger rising with every step she took, hands shaking with barely contained fury that called to her like a moth to a flame.

Rage, she knew, and Maggie welcomed it like an old friend.

She punched in the passcode to the locked metal doors of Ashton's impressive collection of artillery; the lock clicked open with an electronic beep.

The Berettas caught her eye, reminding her of Venice and having Leon by her side. Selecting a Beretta 8000, Maggie loaded the gun and went to the lanes.

The targets from the day before with Tami were still set up. Maggie fired. She sent shot after shot to the target, running out of bullets and replacing the magazine with dexterous ease before firing again.

Grief was a useless emotion. It left her empty and unable to function. Rage was an active emotion, one that fueled her. Three magazines later, the paper target zipped up the lane, and Maggie ripped it off the hanger. A gaping hole sat where the head used to be with not a bullet wasted. Her blood boiled inside her and she gritted her teeth, scrunching the paper into a ball.

Maggie had no idea what kind of life she'd have without Leon. She couldn't even bring herself to imagine what that was going to look like. Getting through the night seemed like an impossible task. She didn't know what she was going to do without him, but she did know one thing.

Maggie was going to do what she should have done back at St. Paul's Cathedral when she discovered the truth about Bishop and his partner in crime.

She was going to kill Nina.

Chapter 9

London, Great Britain
1 5 June

M aggie pulled up to the Unit headquarters in Ashton's sleek black Porsche and parked right up front in the loading bay that was never used. The sign for Inked International hung above to blend in with the surrounding offices on King Street.

The shutters were down on The Golden Lion next door, the old-school pub stirring memories of happier times. Of nights spent laughing and drinking with Leon and her fellow agents to celebrate successful missions and a job well done. Of toasting absent friends who had fallen in the line of duty. And to commiserate with those who'd come back from a harrowing time in the field that didn't go to plan.

Nina and Bishop were part of those memories. They'd been there, all the while stabbing each and every one of them in the back and betraying everything they stood for.

Another day of great weather had greeted London, the perfect summer's morning in direct contrast with the storm building inside Maggie.

She rapped the door until a startled man at the front desk let her in. She glared at him before his request for ID escaped his lips. He knew who she was. Everyone at the Unit did. Had it not been for Maggie, the Unit would have dissolved when Ivan Dalca and his syndicate came for them.

Clenching her teeth to keep her warring emotions in check, Maggie ascended in the elevator like she had done countless times before and got out on the fourth floor. Thankfully, she didn't pass anyone in the hallway. A run-in with an old colleague might break her, unable to stand their sympathies and well wishes or questions about how she was holding up and on the funeral arrangements. Maggie wasn't ready for that. For any of it.

She headed straight for Leon's office where the director general usually took up residence when paying a visit to headquarters. Maggie hovered at the door adorned with Leon's name etched in an engraved silver plaque. Whoever replaced him would have big shoes to fill.

Without knocking, Maggie entered to find Grace at the conference table, Leon's desk deliberately left untouched. A framed photo of them in the flat with Willow sat next to his computer, and Maggie had to look away.

"Maggie, nice of you to make an appointment and wait downstairs for a visitors' pass," Grace said, who, unlike Ashton and Tami, spoke to her like she always did with her no-bullshit, matter-of-fact manner. For that, Maggie was grateful.

She pulled out a chair and sat across from her old boss. "I figured you'd be too busy for any appointments since you have Leon's murder to work and a rogue ex-employee to find."

Grace closed a file she'd been reading and clasped her hands on top of it. "Believe me, I have everyone working on this as we speak. Cup of tea?"

Maggie nodded, noting in true British fashion that no matter the situation, tea seemed to be offered. Nervous about something? Tea will calm your nerves. Ill? Tea will keep you warm. Finished all the housework? Have a nice cuppa in reward. Love of your life murdered in cold blood by an old enemy? Tea.

The kettle boiled in silence and Grace busied herself with laying out cups and collecting the milk from the little fridge underneath the counter in the corner. "Am I allowed to ask how you're holding up?"

"I don't know." Maggie picked at her nails, unable to sit still.

"I was in shock for weeks when I lost my Malcolm," Grace said. She placed a cup down before Maggie, seeming to remember how she liked it, and returned to her seat. "We both knew the cancer would kill him in the end, yet no matter how much I thought I'd prepared myself for the inevitable, you can never be ready for the death of your other half. We were lucky enough to have many long and happy years together, so I won't patronize you and tell you I know how you feel. I can't imagine."

Tears pricked Maggie's eyes, but she willed them not to fall. Crying more than she already had wouldn't help. She'd come here for a reason.

"I assume you've been searching for Nina since the mess last year, yes?"

Since Nina had made a point of announcing her involvement in the theft of the Unit's data and agent list, she had undoubtedly won first position on the agency's most-wanted list. A fact Nina would have anticipated.

"Correct," Helmsley said. "We began investigations into her whereabouts as soon as we cleared up the mess she caused with Ivan Dalca."

"Yet you haven't found her." Maggie fought to stay in control and batted down the building rage that waited to be released with a stirring impatience. "Leon would still be here had you managed to do so."

"Likewise," Grace bit back. "You've had as long as we've had to track her down."

Maggie recoiled like Grace had punched her. It would have hurt less if she had. Again, tears threatened to spill, to show her weakness, which only infuriated her more.

"You have an entire staff and a huge government budget behind you."

Grace's lips thinned. "From what I understand, you and Mr. Price have a firm of your own that deals in this field, so it appears both our efforts have come up short."

The tension grew thick in their silence, neither woman willing to back down. Yet Grace was right. Had Maggie tried harder to track down Nina, this never would have happened. She'd been so wrapped up in being happy and living her life that she'd shoved thoughts of Nina to the side. They'd heard nothing from Nina since she had flowers delivered to Maggie in the hospital with a note promising to see her soon.

A year had gone by without a single word from her, and they'd all assumed she'd backed off to raise her and Bishop's newborn child. Leon had hoped being a mother would put things into perspective for Nina and that she'd give up any idea of revenge toward them for exposing (and ruining) what she and Bishop had been up to.

They were wrong. So wrong.

"Do you have anything?" Maggie asked, desperate for something that would help find Nina. "Any leads at all?"

The Unit had trained them all too well. If Nina didn't want to be found, she was more than capable of avoiding detection until she decided to come out from the shadows again. Grace knew it as much as Maggie did, and it was written all over her face.

"I've told you already, our cases are classified to you now," Helmsley said instead.

Maggie prickled and squeezed her cup so hard, the tea sloshed over the rim, burning her hand. "They weren't classified when you needed me last time."

"That was different. The risks were much higher than they are in this c—"

"I advise you *not* to finish that sentence."

Grace's bodyguards weren't around to hold Maggie at bay, yet to the director general's credit, she didn't react or make for the door. She kept her cool like always, which Maggie had always both hated and admired about the old woman. Say what you want about her, but Grace Helmsley was a tough nut to crack with nerves of steel.

She watched Maggie with calculating eyes. "You could always come back into the fold."

"That will never happen," Maggie replied. Grace had asked before, and time away from the Unit had only solidified Maggie's decision. There was no going back for her. Not now. Not without Leon.

"The Unit needs you now more than ever," Grace pressed, clearly not used to being told no.

Maggie deflated, shoulders drooping as her anger fizzled to leave nothing but sadness. She stared at her cup, her body drained and bone tired in a way she'd never experienced.

"Honestly, Grace, I don't think I'll ever come back from this. I'm barely capable of making it through the next five minutes, never mind think about being an agent again. It's all too much."

Grace put a hand over Maggie's, giving it a squeeze.

"You might not believe this, but Leon meant a great deal to me. As do all my agents, you included. I will not let Nina get away with this. She will pay for what she did to Leon and everything else she's put us all through."

Maggie stared through her curtain of hair to Grace's resolute expression. She meant every word of what she said, and while Helmsley was many things, a liar wasn't one of them. Leon wasn't the only agent Grace had lost because of Nina. She'd almost died herself last year after being abducted by Dalca's men who broke into her house in the middle of the night.

"Thank you, Grace. I'm just not in a place where I can help. I'm afraid I'd be more of a hindrance than anything right now."

Grace patted her hand and returned to her tea. "Sit this one out and grieve. We'll handle it, and I promise I'll let you know when we find her."

"Okay," Maggie said, taking a deep breath. Sitting out had never been a role she played well, and it rarely happened when she was an active agent. She got up to leave.

"One thing before you go," Grace said, her voice wavering for the first time since Maggie had been there. She sat again as Grace searched inside her handbag. "Leon had this in his desk drawer."

She moved a small object across the table, and Maggie picked it up with shaking, trepidatious fingers. The velvet was soft against her skin as she pried open the little box. The diamond winked up at her in jest, surrounded in platinum rather than gold.

Any bravado Maggie had mustered when facing Grace up and left the building as she looked at the jewelry. It blurred before her as tears pooled and spilled down her cheeks.

"A ring?"

Grace cleared her throat, words thick with emotion. "Leon had secured a week off work next month and had arranged a trip to Venice for you both. He planned to ask you then."

Maggie touched the ring for a moment but pulled back as if burned. She snapped the box shut and bowed her head. "Can I have a moment alone, please?"

"Of course." Grace got up and Maggie felt a hand on her shoulder. "I'll be outside if you need me."

The door closed softly, and Maggie waited until she

heard Grace's footsteps walk down the hall. When she was certain the director general was out of earshot, she wiped her face and moved to sit at Leon's desk.

The computer whizzed to life in seconds, and Maggie entered Leon's username—all the agents' logins were based on the same format using their initials, surname, and agent number. The password posed a problem though.

Maggie wasn't as good a hacker as Tami, but she had a few tricks up her sleeve from her training. It took longer than it should have, but Maggie didn't keep up with her tech skills like she should, preferring to punch faces rather than keyboard keys.

Given Leon's clearance level, she had full access once she managed to bypass the password. Searching through the files, Maggie kept an eye on the door, conscious that Grace could walk in at any moment.

File after file, Maggie rummaged through until she found what she was looking for. Each agent was required to leave a next of kin on their file in case of emergencies, and Nina was no exception. Memorizing the address, Maggie clicked the file closed and logged out, turning off the computer and leaving Leon's office with the framed picture of them in hand.

The Unit had trained her well, too, and Maggie had no intentions of leaving it to them to hunt Nina down.

This was personal, and Maggie fully intended to get to the bitch first.

Chapter 10

Belfast, Northern Ireland
16 June

With the address of Nina's mother's house embedded in her memory, Maggie wasted no time in heading straight there. Ashton had insisted he go to the Unit with her to meet Grace, but Maggie convinced him she'd be better going alone, using the fact that he and Grace had a tenuous relationship at best. After she'd failed to return to West Sussex some hours later, her phone rang. And rang.

Instead of picking up and explaining what she was doing, she tossed the phone and headed for the ferry, it being a safer route with less security than traveling by plane. She ditched Ashton's Porsche in a parking spot, making sure to pay for the few days it would take him to track down the vehicle. It'd also keep him busy while she was away.

Maggie had already lost Leon, and she wasn't about to involve Ashton and Tami if she could help it. Better to handle this herself, once and for all. They could chastise her when, or if, she returned.

Having come up through training with Nina, Maggie wasn't stupid enough to underestimate her. Nina was as fierce and as ruthless as they came, and strategic to boot. In the year they'd spent forgetting about her and focused on moving on, Nina had used that time to plan her revenge.

Maggie zipped up her jacket against the wind, Belfast experiencing a more common British summer than London. The small suburb sat a few miles outside the city center and oozed upper-class contentment, with large, neatly tended gardens, twin garages, and houses that each boasted at least five bedrooms. Nina's privileged upbringing had been clear when Maggie first met her, both of them polar opposites at the time, yet equally matched in most of their classes.

Reaching number 32 on the quaint street, Maggie stayed hidden, making use of the high hedges separating each house and the tall trees that branched out in twin rows on either side of the road.

While Maggie was tempted to charge straight in,

Nina could be inside and prepared for such an intrusion. The agent side of Maggie dominated her impatience, and she spent the morning casing the house. Watching. Waiting.

Most of the surrounding houses appeared vacant for the day with people out at work, which made it easier to avoid being spotted by nosy neighbors with too much time on their hands.

Maggie stifled a yawn. While she'd arrived last night, she practically fell into bed at the hotel she'd booked into, too exhausted to stake out the address then. Stalking through the streets of the little suburb at that time wouldn't have gone unnoticed either. Better to approach in the light of day.

Three hours passed, and there'd been no sign of Nina. Maggie spotted who she assumed to be Nina's mother, Fiona, walking past the window of the front room a few times and answering the door to the postman, but there didn't appear to be anyone else home. That didn't mean much, though. If she was laying low at her mother's, Nina would hardly pass by the front windows.

Still, nothing indicated that Fiona had guests. Having snuck into the back garden, Maggie watched her as she made tea for one, stealing a good glance beyond the kitchen and into the dining room in the process.

Time wore on, and Maggie's reserve of patience ran dry. Gun tucked safely at the small of her back, she squared her shoulders and made the approach, keeping an eye out for anything amiss.

Instinct more than anything played a big role in these circumstances. If her gut told her something was off, it was usually right, and this had saved her from some sticky situations out in the field.

Ringing the doorbell, Maggie prepared for anything while plastering a wide smile on an inviting, innocent face. The woman from her watch answered soon after. Up close, the resemblance confirmed Maggie's assumption that she was indeed Nina's mother.

"Hello," she said in a thick Irish accent, still strikingly beautiful for her age. Her chestnut hair was shorter than her daughter's, but she had the same sharp features and lithe frame.

"Hi, I wonder if you could help me. I'm in town for a bit with work and wanted to check in on an old friend from school. Does Nina O'Brien still live here?"

"Oh, how lovely. Yes, this is Nina's home, at least it used to be. I'm her mother, Fiona."

"Nice to meet you," Maggie replied, shaking Fiona's hand. "Is Nina around?"

"I'm afraid not." Fiona opened the door wider and stepped aside. "Do come in though."

"Are you sure? I don't want to impose."

Maggie feigned a shy duck of her head to check either side of her for signs of Nina. She wouldn't put it past her old colleague to use her mother as a distraction to escape or sneak up on Maggie when she least expected it.

"Nonsense!" Fiona said, waving her in. "Any friend of Nina's is welcome anytime."

"Thanks very much," Maggie said, wiping her feet on the doormat and following Fiona inside once she was certain outside was clear. "You have a lovely home."

The house was an older two-story Georgian with high ceilings and large rooms, decorated with a modern yet inviting flare that reminded Maggie of Gillian's place in Cambridge. Creams and pastels played center stage with the odd antique ornament or trinket here and there.

"Thank you—oh, how rude of me. I haven't even asked your name, love."

"It's Maggie," she said, taking an offered seat on the living room couch and shrugging off her jacket. "Maggie Black."

Unlike the many missions she'd carried out before, Maggie had no need for an alias here. She wanted Nina to know she'd found her family. That she could reach Nina's loved ones too.

"Nice to meet you, Maggie. Would you like some tea or coffee?"

"Tea would be great, thanks."

As soon as Fiona shuffled off to the kitchen, Maggie was on her feet, leaning against the wall by the door and inching her head around to scan the hallway, fingers brushing her gun. Creeping out of the living room, she tiptoed to the stairs and peered up, watching and listening for any sign of a houseguest.

"What do you take in your tea?" Fiona called through.

"Milk, please," Maggie replied, debating if she had enough time to carry out a quick search upstairs before the woman returned. Instead of risking it, Maggie slinked back to her seat as Fiona came from the kitchen with a tea tray and a plate of scones.

A knife sat on the tray next to the jam. Not sharp, but nothing a little force couldn't fix.

Luckily for Fiona O'Brien, Maggie hadn't come to take her insatiable need for payback out on anyone other than her wretched daughter. It'd be so easy to take the woman out. To snap her fragile neck or put a bullet in her brain. To leave a clear message written in spilled blood like Nina had.

"So, you know my Nina from Westbrook Academy?" Fiona asked, pouring milk in Maggie's tea and handing her the cup.

"Yes, we were in the same graduating class."

They all were. Maggie, Nina, Ashton, and Leon. And while Westbrook was an academy of sorts, the education they each received there had been a bit more specialized than your average school. Instead of geography and home economics, they attended lessons in espionage and deception. While most teenagers studied for their GCSEs,

Maggie and the others endured countless hours of martial arts training, and their exams were literally life or death.

A shudder ran through Maggie at the memories of being tortured, an important part of any agent's training to test their ability to stay silent and not leak intelligence, no matter how dire the circumstances.

Fiona sipped her tea. "Nina loved it there. Far more than her other boarding school, let me tell you."

"I remember her telling me about being suspended a few times," Maggie said, recalling when she'd been stupid enough to believe Nina was her friend.

Scouts on the hunt for the next generation of Unit agents searched for a very particular type to join the ranks. While Nina never admitted to killing her teacher, nor had any evidence pointed toward her since the police deemed it a terrible accident, she'd managed to land herself on Bishop's radar. He recruited her a few months before he found Maggie.

Fiona shook her head. "She's always been a handful, that one. Too smart for her own good."

She made to offer Maggie a scone when a cry carried into the room from upstairs.

"That'll be Cara awake, then," Fiona said, getting up.

Maggie frowned. "Cara?" She inched forward on her seat, hands ready to grab her gun at a moment's notice.

"Nina's little one. I'll be right back."

The stairs creaked as Fiona went upstairs. A few

minutes later, she returned with a baby in her arms. Despite her earlier cries, the little one was all smiles now.

"She's had a bit of a cold, haven't you, missy?" Fiona cooed, kissing the girl's forehead.

"She's beautiful," Maggie said when Fiona sat back down with Cara on her lap. The baby watched her with interest, tiny hands holding on to her grandmother's blouse. She couldn't be more than eight or nine months old, with chubby cheeks and hazel eyes.

"I know," Fiona said, beaming with pride, "and the double of her mother at that age too."

"Are you minding her for the day?" Maggie didn't mind waiting for Nina to come back for Cara. While she'd never hurt the child or Fiona, Maggie wouldn't make the same mistake again and let her heartstrings be tugged at the fact Nina had become a mother.

Nina deserved to die, and Maggie intended to make sure it was by her own hands. And soon.

Sooner than expected, perhaps, if Nina was coming back to pick up Cara.

Fiona fumbled over her words for a second, shifting a wriggling Cara in her arms. "No, I've had her since she came out of the hospital."

"Oh?" Maggie said, deflating at the news but making sure to hide it.

"Nina stayed for a bit, but she just couldn't bond with the little one." Fiona's face flushed, like she was embarrassed to admit it. "I tried to make her stay, but

Nina's never listened to anything I say, even when she was a child herself. Too much like her bloody father."

Memories of sitting in the doctor's office rose their ugly head. Of being told she'd lost Leon's baby and collapsing to the floor as the news hit her harder than any punch could. Now she'd lost Leon too.

Cara giggled as she listened to them chat, cooing and babbling to join in. Sitting before Nina's baby caused needles of guilt to stab into Maggie's side, knowing her actions would leave this innocent, joyful little girl without a mother. Though, from what Fiona was saying, Nina hadn't been much of a mother to begin with.

"Listen to me, going on," Fiona said, eyes glistening. "I'm sorry."

Maggie placed a reassuring hand on Fiona's knee. "Don't be. I'm sure it's been hard on you. Was something wrong? With Nina, I mean."

Nina had this beautiful baby waiting here for her, and instead she'd chosen to take the second chance at life Maggie had given her and put her energy into ruining Maggie's future. Into ripping her world apart when she should be here, spending time with Cara. Revenge mattered more to Nina than this little girl did.

"Postpartum depression, I suspect," Fiona said. "I tried to get her to talk to me, or Reverend Quinn down at the church, but she can be so secretive. She even refused to tell me who the father was. You don't happen to know if she'd been seeing anyone?"

Brice Bishop.

Little Cara already had one dead parent. By the time Maggie had finished, both would be gone. While she took no joy in the thought, Maggie's mission hadn't changed. Nina was as good as dead, and she'd stop at nothing to end her.

"I must admit, I've not seen much of Nina for a while now," Maggie said. "I wish I could help."

Nothing good would come from Fiona learning who Cara's father was.

Fiona hid the flash of disappointment from her face and busied herself with fixing Cara's pink socks from slipping off her feet. "Not to worry. I'll look after this one until Nina comes back. It's so nice to have a baby in the house again. I'm loving it."

Cara laughed as Fiona tickled her, the grandmother's love for her granddaughter clear as day.

"Have you heard from Nina lately?" Maggie asked, her untouched tea turning cold as her only lead dried up before her.

"She texts now and again, but not as often as a mother would like. I hope you don't neglect your own mother like that."

Maggie reached for her locket. "My mum died when I was little."

"Sorry to hear that," Fiona said, her kind nature catching Maggie off guard.

While Nina had inherited her physical features from

her mother, Maggie couldn't see a single personality trait shared by mother and daughter. Nina had clearly gotten her vindictiveness from her abusive father, whom Fiona had divorced not long after Maggie and Nina had completed their first official job out in the field.

"You said you were over here for work?"

"Yes, my office is in London, but I travel a lot on business."

"And a workaholic like Nina, no doubt. You couldn't pry her away from her phone or laptop. Even the last time she was here."

Who could Nina be on the phone with? Had she planned Leon's murder while staying with her mother? Made her arrangements to return to London for that very reason? The urge to get up and leave tugged at Maggie, but she stayed put. She still needed information. Something to go on, no matter how small.

"When was that? Have I missed her by much?"

"Oh, a good few months ago, now," Fiona said, just before her mobile rang. "That will be Siobhan from the choir. I forgot to ring her this morning about sheet music. Here, hold Cara for me while I get it."

Cara was in Maggie's arms before she could object, staring up at her with big, tentative eyes. Fiona stepped into the hallway to take her phone call while Maggie sat there, unsure what to do.

"Hello," she said, which resulted in an excited reply from Cara, speaking fluent baby. Her hand wrapped around Maggie's fingers and a crushing pain ached in Maggie's chest. She'd never have this now. That, too, had been taken from her.

Nina had stolen a lifetime of possibilities from Maggie in one fell swoop. Instead of reveling in what she had, of the miracle sitting on Maggie's lap right now, Nina had chosen to ruin Maggie's life.

Of all the mistakes Nina had made, killing Leon was the one that would get her killed.

"Sorry about that," Fiona said, phone call ended. "Siobhan is in a tizzy over our next performance."

Fiona placed her phone on the table by the tea and Maggie got to her feet, handing Cara back. "I best be going," she said, gathering her jacket. Hand hidden, she brushed against the table and swiped Fiona's phone, slipping the device into her pocket. "Thanks for the tea, Ms. O'Brien. It was nice meeting you."

"You too, dear," Fiona said, none the wiser as Cara helpfully distracted her. "Come back anytime."

Maggie said her goodbyes and left with conflicted emotions. While she didn't take pride in making a baby an orphan, at least Cara had a loving grandmother with the time, want, and means to take good care of her. Unlike Maggie, Cara wouldn't be put into care to live with strangers.

She took one last look at the house, knowing she'd never be back.

And neither would Nina.

Chapter 11

Someone followed her. She could feel it. Eyes watching her from behind, tailing her movements as she left Fiona's house and continued down the street.

Maggie kept her casual pace, never once looking over her shoulder. The longer her stalker believed she was unaware of their presence, the better.

The Beretta at her back called for her, but she didn't dare reach for it. Not yet.

Her heartbeat pulsed in her ears, muscles tense and ready for a fight. Had Ms. O'Brien lied to her? Covered for Nina while she prepared to attack? Lured Maggie into a false sense of security with a welcoming demeanor and lies of not knowing Nina's whereabouts? Had they sunk as low as to use baby Cara as a distraction?

Maggie didn't put it past them. Not after everything Nina had done.

The street stretched out agonizingly long, making it feel like an eternity to reach the crossroad that led off in three different directions. Sticking to the left-hand side, Maggie walked around the hedges squaring off the house at the end of the neighborhood and crept along to the bottom of the back garden, making the most of the precious head start to duck behind the eight-foot, ivy-covered fence.

Light footsteps followed close behind, speeding up upon Maggie's disappearance. Gun in her hand, Maggie waited, pricking her ears as the footsteps grew louder, holding for the perfect moment to strike.

As her stalker approached her hiding spot, Maggie jumped out from behind the fence, clotheslining her pursuer in the neck and sending them crashing to the ground. Maggie pounced before he had time to react. The wind knocked from the man's chest with an audible exhale upon landing as she pointed the Beretta in his face. His familiar face.

"Bloody hell, Ash. I could have shot you."

"And with my own gun too," Ashton said with a groan.

Maggie tucked the Beretta away and got to her feet, holding a hand out for her friend. "How did you find me?"

"Tami tracked your phone," Ashton said, dusting off his clothes.

"I dumped my phone."

Ashton winked at her. "Not your burner."

"How do you even know about my burner?" Maggie pinched the bridge of her nose. "You know what, never mind. What are you doing here?"

Ashton folded his arms, towering over her. "What are *you* doing here?"

Maggie pointed a thumb behind them. "Nina's mum lives there."

"I gathered as much when Tami ran the address and we got the name of the houseowner. The girl can hack like nobody's business, I'll give her that."

They walked away, the wind picking up and blowing Maggie's blond hair back. Above, gray clouds congregated, dimming the day as they blocked the sun.

Maggie could kick herself about the burner. Ashton was sly as a fox, and with Tami helping out, Maggie knew they might have been able to track her movements, but she'd hoped they'd at least be one step behind her—and out of the way of Nina's wrath—in the process. If Maggie kept Nina busy, she'd have no time to set her eyes on her friends.

"Was that Nina's kid you were holding?" Ashton asked, his long legs slowing to match her gait.

"A little girl named Cara. Nina up and left her with her mum."

"And you up and left me and Tami," Ashton accused, rounding on Maggie as his voice rose. "You had us worried sick."

"I'm sorry, but I need to do this." Maggie walked around him and continued down the street.

Ashton caught up with ease, his brow furrowed and jaw set. "Do what? What's the plan here, Mags?"

"I'm going to kill her. She needs to be stopped."

If Maggie ditched the gun, she could catch a flight instead of taking the ferry back to London. It'd save time, and she could stop by the flat to collect her Glock and other weapons she and Leon had kept there.

If she had the strength to go back, that is. Even the idea of stepping inside their apartment had her hands shaking.

Did the Unit still have the flat cordoned off? Had they cleaned the bloody sheets and rose petals, or had they left them there to wilt and wither away like Maggie's heart? She guessed she'd find out.

Ashton seized her arm and yanked her back from charging ahead. "She does need to be stopped, but you're not doing this alone."

Maggie shoved him away and glared. "I don't want anyone else to get hurt. I can't lose another person."

"Neither can I," Ashton said, shouting now. He never shouted at her. "You're not the only one who lost Leon. He was our family, too, and we're all hurting."

"It's better this way," Maggie said, trying to make him see sense. "This is my fight."

"It's *our* fight. Jesus Christ, Maggie. I'm fed up telling you that you're not alone. We're in this together. Leon told you the same thing. I thought we were over this shit."

"This is different," Maggie said, shouting now too. "Leon's *dead*. Nina won't stop with him. She's left her and Bishop's child here to come at us."

Being unable to bond with her child was one thing, but Nina had left Cara in the loving care of Fiona, knowing her daughter would be safe, and as far as Nina was aware, hidden. To have left her baby and walked away knowing she might never return told Maggie that Nina meant business. She'd stop at nothing to ruin Maggie's life and get her revenge.

"Us," Ashton corrected, still following her. "To come at *us*. Running off alone won't stop Nina from targeting the rest of us. You know that."

Rain scattered the ground and turned to heavy within seconds, drenching them both.

"It's me she wants most," Maggie insisted. Once they found each other, only one of them would walk away. Either Maggie would be successful, or Nina will get her prime target and go back to being invisible and staying off the Unit's radar. "Nina won't lay a finger on any of you if I get to her first."

"And how is that working out for you?" Ashton said, his black hair stuck to his face. "I've had to leave Tami with Gillian to follow you here. Who's looking after them right now?"

Nauseating worry overcame Maggie. While Ashton wouldn't have left them helpless, both Tami and Gillian would be safer with him around. For all Maggie knew, Nina had been watching them for months. Ever since she left Fiona and Cara. Perhaps before then, if she had people do her dirty work for her. She'd know all about Gillian and Tami if she'd been keeping tabs on Maggie.

It dawned on her that Nina had turned up on the one night Maggie wasn't home. The staged scene with the rose petals had been thought out. Planned in advance. She hadn't considered it until now, too lost in the shock of it all to pay closer attention to the details. Nina hadn't planned on coming for them both that night, only to find Leon. She knew Maggie wouldn't be there.

"You shouldn't have come," Maggie told Ashton, more worried for Tami and Gillian now than ever.

Ashton pulled out a set of keys from his jacket and a car beeped to life across the street. "Get in the car."

"No," Maggie said, the rain getting heavier.

Nina had poisoned Leon to avoid a fight with him. They all knew each other's strengths and weaknesses, but even Maggie would have had a hard time standing toe to toe with Leon. His size and sheer strength were a brutal combination given his skill level and ability to keep a cool head.

Instead, Nina took the sly route and drugged him.

Adding her concoction to the pizza Leon ordered that night, or in one of his beers, most likely. She always liked using poisons, reveled too much in their effects and the slow, painful deaths most of them brought.

"Maggie, get in the fucking car," Ashton yelled, standing by the driver's door.

She didn't budge. "Are you going to try to make me?"

"If I need to, because I'm not leaving you to do this alone."

Her clothes clung to her as raindrops ran down her face. "He was going to ask me to marry him, Ash."

Ashton's Adam's apple bobbed as he fought back emotion. "I know. He told me a few weeks ago. He was so excited."

Of course, Ashton knew. He and Leon were inseparable, making up for the years of friendship and brotherhood they'd lost since Ashton left the Unit.

"It doesn't feel real," Maggie said. "I keep expecting to wake up and discover it was all one big horrible nightmare. I was so happy, Ash."

Ashton crossed the street again and pulled her to him. "I know."

"If I stop now, I'll break," she admitted, barely able to get the words out. "I'll be useless, and I can't afford the time to grieve while Nina's still out there. I need to stop her."

Ashton looked down at her, deep blue eyes pleading. "Then come home with me and we'll do this together.

The way Leon would have wanted. We're a team, and this is exactly the kind of thing we created Engage for. Consider this our first case."

"And then what? If we manage to survive this, what then?"

Even thinking about waking up without Leon lying next to her left a vacant hole in her chest. Most of her hopes and dreams, the ones that mattered most, included him. She'd taken it for granted that they'd be by each other's side until they were gray and old. Her heart ached, not only about Leon's death but for the years of happiness they'd had in front of them. For the life they would have shared.

"What am I going to do?" she asked again, at a total loss.

Ashton led her to the car and opened the passenger-side door. "We'll figure that out when the time comes. For now, let's focus on doing what we do best."

"It's not going to be easy," Maggie said, all of the fight in her washed away with the rain.

The door closed and Ashton hopped in on his side, starting the engine of the rental car and pulling out onto the road.

"It never is."

Chapter 12

London, Great Britain
17 June

Maggie stood at the end of the conference table in their Mayfair office, the expectant faces of Tami, Gillian, and Ashton staring back at her. They'd arrived back in London late last evening and spent the night at Ashton's penthouse a few streets away instead of returning to the estate in West Sussex.

Tami and Gillian met them at Engage twenty minutes ago, having driven down from Gillian's house in Cambridge. From the dark bags under their eyes, they'd gotten about as much sleep as Maggie. Sleeping didn't come easy without Leon lying next to her. She reached over for him in her drowsy state multiple times during the night only to find Leon's side empty.

"Thanks for coming," Maggie said. "You all know why we're here."

Gillian nodded, and Maggie's heart stung at the pity behind her friend's eyes. "We'll help in any way we can, love."

Walking over to the glass panel, Maggie stuck a headshot of Nina next to her circled name. Hate boiled inside Maggie for the woman looking back, the hint of a smirk edging at her old colleague's lips. She wouldn't be smiling for long.

"Our first target is Nina O'Brien. The last official sighting of her was last June at St. John's Cathedral. At the time, she was around sixteen weeks pregnant and I let her escape before the Unit arrived to apprehend her."

Maggie searched each of her friends' faces for judgment but found none. Had she handed Nina over, Leon would still be here. While her decision had more to do with the unborn child than Nina, Maggie would never make that mistake again. Moments of weakness like that were over, and she would spare no mercy to the woman who assassinated her partner.

"We treat this like any other case," Maggie said, trying to ignore the shake in her voice. "We leave no stone unturned. Nina is highly skilled, ruthless, and has planned her attack on us for months. She has the ability to execute the most intricate of jobs and was the top choice at the Unit for wet work."

"Psychotic bitch," Ashton said, his words laced with venom.

"Is she psychotic?" Tami asked, taking notes on her laptop without needing to peer down at the keys. "Clinically, I mean?"

Maggie shrugged. "She passed the psych evaluation back when she was recruited."

The doctor who carried out their tests had quizzed Maggie for hours on end, paying special interest to the night she'd taken her first life, the only murder she'd committed up to that point. A few years with the Unit soon brought that tally to a number Maggie refused to calculate, yet of all the lives she'd ended, she could never bring herself to feel guilty over the one that started it all. Monsters like that man had it coming.

Ashton scoffed. "Even I passed that psych eval, which says everything."

"I doubt Bishop cared much about the results," Maggie admitted, fidgeting with the lid of a red dry-erase pen. "He wanted young people he could train and mold into cold-blooded killers. That was his priority, and Nina never had any issue ending a life, even before she became an agent."

Maggie was no better, yet her reasons for taking action were far different from Nina's. Maggie had never meant for things to go that far, the situation escalating beyond her control and forcing her hand. Unlike Nina, who had planned her first kill. Much like she'd planned Leon's death too.

Gillian leaned back in her chair and stared at Nina's photo. Neither she nor Tami had met Nina, though Tami had suffered as a result of her actions "You know her more than most, Maggie. What can you tell us about her?"

"So much of what I thought I knew turned out to be a lie," Maggie admitted. "I thought she was our friend. I trusted her. I feel like an idiot now, but looking back, both she and Bishop had been so careful to hide what they were doing. They ran their operation like the spies they were, and they did a good job concealing it from the rest of us."

Until Bishop made the mistake of trying to have Maggie killed. She'd gotten too close to the truth, had investigated a case more thoroughly than he'd expected, only to reveal the real enemy, both of whom were under the Unit's own roof.

Maggie had tried so hard to put the past behind her, to bury it and start her new life with Leon. Yet the past had come back to bite her, and Nina's vengeance ripped scabs off wounds Maggie believed to be healed.

"Why don't you start from the beginning?" Tami said. "Let's map out her life and look for areas we can use to our advantage."

"I knew we hired you for a reason," Ashton said, shooting Tami an approving wink.

Tami smiled at her mentor's praise, and they all turned to Maggie once again. She froze under their stare for a moment as a flash intruded of Bishop taking the helm at a Unit meeting not unlike this one. They were all there—Maggie, Leon, Ashton, and Nina. Eager new recruits fresh out of training and ready to prove themselves. Even then, Nina held on to Bishop's every word.

Two of them were dead now, and regardless of who emerged victorious from Maggie and Nina's battle, a third would be joining them soon.

Maggie gave herself a shake and pulled her attention back to the present.

"I met Nina the first day I arrived at Westbrook Academy, a Unit training facility that masqueraded as a small private school. It was a pet project of Bishop's, taking in teenagers with promise and fashioning them into killers through a rigorous education in key areas required for the job."

"Spy school," Ashton said, getting up and fixing himself a coffee. He spiked it with the contents of his silver flask, but Maggie didn't say anything. They all had their ways of coping. "Sounds cooler than it actually was. We'd all been there for about a month before Mags arrived to show us all up. Nina didn't like that."

"She was competitive?" Gillian asked, the letters of

her name gleaming from a polished name tag pinned to her pink cardigan.

"At first. Bishop encouraged it among us all, to keep us focused and striving to be better. We became friends soon enough though. We all did."

"Some sooner than others," Ashton said, his playful smile replaced with a sincere warmth he rarely showed those outside of his close circle. He'd been the youngest of them all, not to mention the smartest. Too smart for his own good sometimes, and he hadn't made the best impression with the others before Maggie turned up. She had liked him instantly, with his bad attitude and reluctance to take their military-style regimen seriously.

"Each of us were handpicked for different reasons. Leon had displayed promise as a young army recruit."

Ashton laughed. "I blew up the science wing of my school."

Gillian giggled while Tami's eyes widened. "By accident?" she asked.

Ashton arched an eyebrow.

"How did you get recruited?" Gillian asked, sobering.

"That's a story for another time," Maggie said. Few people knew her story, and she liked to keep it that way. She folded her arms and paced while she spoke. "Nina, on the other hand, had been in the center of a scandal at a private school in Londonderry."

"Shagging her French teacher," Ashton added. "Guess she's always had a thing for older men."

Maggie shivered at the thought. She'd always looked up to Bishop as a father figure, which she had severely lacked growing up. To think Nina viewed him as anything else felt wrong. They had been sixteen when they were recruited. Kids.

"When the teacher decided to end things with Nina, she blackmailed him to stay together," Maggie continued. "Eventually, he grew tired of it and called things off for good. Nina made a show of exposing their relationship, including to the man's fiancée, and things got worse from there."

"How?" Tami asked over the clack of her keys.

Maggie pulled out a chair and sat, too weary to stand. "Two weeks later, the French teacher was found dead of a supposed drug overdose. He had a suicide letter clutched in his hand, professing his love for Nina and shunning the fiancée."

Gillian got up and shuffled over to fix herself a cup of tea, flicking on the kettle. "Bishop recruited her for blackmailing someone?" she asked, like a mum asking her kid how their day was.

"No, she killed the guy," Ashton said, knocking back his Irish coffee. "Had plans to off the fiancée too."

Nina had never divulged if she forged the letter herself, or if she'd forced the man to write it before he died. She'd been so nonchalant when she told Maggie the story back in training, as if she was recounting some funny story about her time living in the school dorms.

Maggie hadn't been quick to judge, despite her unease. At the time, she was still processing the fact she'd murdered a man too. Nina had made light of the situation to avoid really thinking about it. Or so Maggie had thought.

"The police questioned Nina, but the evidence pointed to the obvious. It got flagged at the Unit as a potential lead, and Bishop went over to meet her before she moved on to the fiancée. After Nina accepted his offer to attend Westbrook, all it took was the proposal of a place at an elite new school and her parents were all too glad to agree."

Gillian crossed the room and put a hot cup of tea down in front of Maggie, giving her back a reassuring rub. "She admitted to killing him?"

"Not to the authorities." Nina would have been happy to tell Bishop, ever eager to please and impress him, even in the early days.

"I'm not a doctor, but I'm going to add 'psychotic' to my notes anyway," Tami said.

"It's possible," Maggie mused, cupping her mug. Even in the hot summer morning, Maggie felt cold all over. A chill she couldn't quite get rid of. "Mental issues affect us all, and her upbringing could explain a lot. Nina grew up in a physically and mentally abusive household. Her dad beat her mother, almost to the point of death at one point. She said this went on for years, both Nina and her mother Fiona on the receiving end. Fiona filed for divorce and pressed charges against her husband when Nina was a young teenager. They settled out of court on both accounts, Fiona walking away with a substantial percentage of her husband's family wealth, but my guess is the damage was already done with Nina."

Gillian shook her head. "Her father created a monster."

"I think she was born bad," Ashton said, brows furrowed as he glared up at Nina's photo.

"Or a mixture of the two," Tami said. "Sounds like a perfect storm to me."

Maggie ran a hand through her hair. "Regardless, Nina displayed a ruthless abandon for the lives of others and a deadly cunning to match. She staged her teacher's death down to the finest details, just like she did with Leon. That kind of meticulous planning involves patience. Nina struck at the right time and place. She's been waiting to make her move, watching and biding her time for the opportune moment."

Gillian stopped mid bite into a chocolate digestive. "Do you think she knows about Engage?"

"Yes," Maggie said. "At the very least, she knew I wouldn't be home that night." *She could be watching right now,* Maggie thought, eyeing the windows and rooftops across the street. "There's no telling how much she knows about us, so I need everyone on high alert. Don't underestimate her."

Ashton's eyes grew dark. "I can take her."

Maggie slammed the desk, causing Tami and Gillian to jump. "I mean it, Ash. This isn't a game."

Nina didn't stand toe to toe with Leon. She knew how that would have gone. So much of her wet work relied on stealth and subtler measures than what Maggie preferred. While she tackled things head-on with fists raised, Nina kept to the shadows, preferring knives in the back and slow poisons.

Ashton might be taller and larger than the lithe and nimble Nina, but Maggie had her doubts Ashton would prove victorious against the woman. She was the perfect agent, skilled and efficient in what she did. Perhaps better than Maggie herself.

While Maggie once considered Nina a friend, Nina had no qualms about framing her for murder. She'd even chased her down while on the run, coming to tie off the loose ends of her and Bishop's schemes, but Maggie had managed to get away. Barely.

Maggie knew now that the real Nina would never have let her leave St. John's Cathedral alive had the shoe been on the other foot. Nina would have slit her throat and thought nothing of it. It was that difference that set them apart. The same difference that could get Maggie killed.

"I know it's not a game," Ashton retorted, stabbing a finger at Nina's photo. "But that one there is going to suffer for what she's done."

"She will," Maggie promised. "But I'll be the one to

cause it. Not you. You hear me? This might be *our* fight, but *I'm* going to be the one to face her."

Looking at her friends, the few people she had left, Maggie made a silent vow to keep all of them out of danger as much as possible. Running off hadn't helped, and the three of them would only follow her if she attempted it again, but she would try to keep them out of things as much as possible.

They could help, and Maggie knew she was going to need all the help she could get to make it through, but she would be the one to die if it came to it. She would take the risks and suffer the consequences of going up against Nina. It was their fight, woman to woman, and only one of them would remain standing by the time they were finished.

Ashton held up his hands, the rage simmering down under her stare. "Sorry, Mags. I'm just venting. I don't know how to take any of this."

"None of us do," Tami said, eyes welling like Ashton's. "How do we intend to take on someone like Nina?"

"Know thy enemy, kiddo," Ashton said, clearing his throat.

Maggie nodded. "He's right. We know Nina. Trained with her. Fought beside her on Unit missions. While she is one of the best, no one is without their flaws. She has a vindictive streak that makes her impulsive. It rarely posed a problem when out on a job since she was detached from her targets. This time, it's personal, and if we push her buttons enough, she'll make a mistake. Hopefully one that can help us track her down."

"What's our first move, then, boss?" Gillian asked.

Maggie pulled out Fiona O'Brien's phone from her pocket and placed it on the desk before them.

"I think this is a good start."

Chapter 13

Maggie slid the phone across the desk to Tami.

"Think you can hack into this? It has a password." Maggie had tried a few times to surpass the locked phone, but her attempts hadn't resulted in much more than frustration.

"Give me a few minutes," Tami said, rummaging through her bag. She pulled out a USB cable and connected the phone to her laptop.

"Whose phone is it?" Gillian asked, sitting to Tami's right.

"Nina's mother's," Maggie said, getting up again and pacing the room, her tea untouched. Every fiber of her being itched to do something, to stay busy before her emotions barged through the facade of keeping herself together. "I swiped it when paying her a visit."

Tami worked away at her laptop, fingers moving at top speed. "There doesn't appear to be any initial security, other than the standard, which is to say, not much at all."

"Can you bypass it?" Ashton asked, on his feet now too.

Tami laughed. "Please."

Maggie stood behind Tami and watched her work her magic. "You'll have to teach me how you do all this one of these days."

"It's not as hard as fighting or shooting a gun."

"I don't know so about that." While not a complete technophobe, Maggie had not excelled in hacking back in training and had relied on the Unit techs more than she liked to admit for that kind of stuff. Getting an intellectual upgrade on the subject from Tami might be prudent.

"We can trade lessons," Tami said, quickly adding, "when you're ready to start them up again, of course."

"Sure," Maggie said, plastering on a quick smile before turning away. Maggie didn't know if she'd ever be able to go back to the way things were. Everything had changed, yet none of it felt real. She kept expecting Leon to walk through the door, or to call to check in on her. He always knew when she was having a bad day, so attuned to her emotions that he could sometimes tell something was wrong before she even realized it herself.

"All right, I'm in," Tami announced, pulling Maggie back into the room and out of her head.

"Go through and search for anything to do with Nina," Maggie said, back to pacing. "She might have left her baby with Fiona, but I don't believe she'd cut off all ties. She'd call to check in when she could at the very least."

There had been real fear in Nina's eyes that night in St. Paul's Cathedral. It wasn't fear of her own death; Nina had never been afraid to die. Maggie had to believe that there was some human part left of her old colleague. A mother's love. Even if she couldn't be the mother little Cara deserved.

"No mention of Nina in the list of contacts," Tami said after a few tense minutes of silence. "Though I doubt someone like her would allow her mother a direct line that could be traced. Not when she's planned her attack on us so thoroughly."

Gillian put on her reading glasses and narrowed her eyes at the laptop screen, which displayed the contents of Fiona's phone. "Perhaps she has her daughter stored under a false name. That's what my Howard does with his fancy woman. Thinks I don't know, but I doubt 'Steve from work' is messaging him photos of his boobs."

Ashton stared at Maggie and they both laughed. It felt absurd to laugh in the middle of everything, but it was so unexpected, yet so *Gillian*, it caught Maggie off guard.

A bite of guilt quickly sank its teeth into her, and she sobered. This was no laughing matter.

"She doesn't have many contacts stored," Tami said, sifting through the information stored in the phone so fast, Maggie had trouble keeping up. "Let me cross-reference them to the names registered under those phone numbers."

Gillian got up from beside her, tea in hand, and crossed the room to the newly installed computers. "While Tami's doing that, I'm going to whip you up some new identities. If Nina has been planning her attack for months, she may already know about the old ones I made you. It shouldn't take too long."

"Good idea," Maggie said. "Do you need anything from me?"

"No, dear, I already have your pictures. I can make any necessary tweaks that need editing on this," Gillian said, patting the monitor. "These are really top-notch. I will need to go home and print them for you, though."

Ashton shook his head and handed Gillian a credit card. "Order new printers along with anything else you need and have them delivered here. Today, if possible. And can you make some for all of us? Something tells me we're going to need them."

They quietened at that. There was no telling what Nina had planned, and she'd already taken one of them out. For all they knew, plans could already be in motion for targeting each of them. None of them were safe, and they wouldn't be as long as Nina still breathed.

"Of course," Gillian said, stepping out of the room to make some calls.

Tami sighed in frustration. "All of the contacts check out and none of her emails or text messages appear to be between her and Nina either. Most of her correspondence is between a group of friends from her local church and choir group. That and a few doctor's appointments for the baby in her calendar."

"Keep looking," Maggie said. This was all they had. There had to be something. Anything they could use.

"You okay?" Ashton asked her, keeping his voice low.

What a loaded question. "I'll be fine," she lied, unable to meet his eyes.

Ashton placed a hand on her shoulder. "You haven't eaten anything today. Want me to go get you something?"

Maggie broke away and crossed her arms. "No, we need to stay together. It's not safe to be alone right now."

Nina could be anywhere.

"I'll get us all something delivered in," Ashton replied, not waiting for an answer. He rang up the café from down the street and placed their usual order. The very café they'd all ordered from when they first got the keys to the place, Leon by their side and thrilled for her and Ashton at making the first steps to set up Engage.

"What do we have here?" Tami said.

Anticipation stirred in Maggie's gut. "What is it?"

"There's an app installed with an encryption feature for messaging. It's been made to look like a bingo app, but the file size is nowhere near the amount required for a game. Sneaky."

Ashton sneered. "Smells like Nina to me. Who's Fiona been messaging on it?"

"I can't tell. No records are kept, and the software ensures everything gets deleted a few seconds after a message is read. It's impossible to tell."

Maggie pulled up a chair next to Tami. "How does it work?"

"It appears to be a two-way system. There isn't a feature to send to a specific person, so I can only conclude that the messages are between two linked phones. Someone else must have the app downloaded and synced with this one."

"Do you think it's her?" Ashton asked.

Maggie picked up the phone, still connected to the laptop. "Only one way to find out."

"Wait," Tami said, eyes wide. "What are you going to say?"

"I don't know yet."

Tami thought for a moment. "If you can get her to call instead of using the app, I might be able to trace the location."

"Won't she have it blocked?" Maggie may not be an expert, but even she knew how to block a phone from being traced given time and the right equipment. If only she'd thought about that with the burner she thought Ashton didn't know about. Then she could be hunting

Nina alone and keeping her remaining loved ones out of harm's way.

"I expect so," Tami said, "but I may be able to get through."

Maggie peered down at the phone and brought up the false bingo app. Her thumbs hovered over the message box. She needed something brief and concise that required an immediate reply. Thinking back to her visit in Dublin, Maggie typed.

CALL ME. SOMETHING'S WRONG WITH CARA.

Maggie hit Send and waited.

"She's not responding," she said after five agonizing minutes passed, gripping the phone tight. Maggie almost resent the message when a response finally came through.

WHAT'S WRONG?

Maggie made to send another message, but Ashton held out a hand. "Don't reply. Just wait."

She complied, and another message came in less than sixty seconds later.

WHAT'S WRONG?

"Wait her out," Ashton said.

"What if she gets spooked?" Tami asked.

This could be the mistake they needed. Maggie watched the screen, willing the anonymous message writer to out themselves. To reveal what her gut screamed at her. "She's panicking. Let's see what she does."

Fiona's phone buzzed in Maggie's hand.

Someone was calling.

Maggie let it ring a few turns before answering and brought the phone to her ear.

"Mam, what's wrong? Is Cara okay?" came a familiar voice.

"Nina," Maggie said, relishing the fear in Nina's voice. "So nice of you to call."

Tami and Ashton froze and listened in with bated breath.

"Are they alive?" Nina asked, her tone deadly cold.

Maggie leaned back in her chair. "For now, at least, which is more than fair of me, considering the circumstances."

"What do you want?"

"What I wanted was to get married to the love of my life and live happily ever after, but you saw to that now, didn't you." Maggie's hands shook, hearing Nina on the other end igniting the pent-up feelings that were ready to burst from her chest in a fiery rage.

"If you lay a finger on either of them, I'm going to—"

"To what?" Maggie snapped. "Kill me? Isn't that what all this is about anyway?"

"Call it payback for what you did."

The hate was mutual, every word that left Nina's mouth filled with the same vitriol that burned inside Maggie.

"What *I* did? You and Bishop were the ones who tried to have me killed."

"I won't fail this time," Nina said with a clear and unsettling shift in her tone. "Just wanted you to suffer a little before the inevitable."

"Careful, Nina," Maggie warned. "You don't want to make me mad, do you? Not when I'm around the little one."

While the lies slipped out with ease, she'd never stoop to Nina's level. She'd never hurt Fiona or little Cara to get back at her. There were lines she refused to cross, and hurting the innocents had never been an option for her.

Nina let out a mocking laugh. "Hurting children now? You wouldn't do that. You don't have it in you."

Considering Maggie's lies about having her family held hostage, Nina didn't do much to temper their conversation.

"You have no idea what I'm capable of. Not now. I allowed little Cara here the chance to be born. I gave you an out, a second chance to get away from it all and raise your daughter, but you shit all over that."

Maggie was yelling now, but she didn't care. The urge to smash and rip and break fumed within.

"You killed my daughter's father," Nina retorted, shouting back at her. "The man I loved."

"He jumped," Maggie said. "He knew it was over and took his own life like the coward he was. I wanted him to rot in prison for what he did. For what you both did."

Regardless of what Maggie wanted, the Unit would

have ever allowed Brice Bishop to be locked away in a cell. He knew just as well as every Unit employee that he would be eliminated. The government agency couldn't afford to allow him to live. The risk of exposure was too high, and Bishop couldn't be trusted not to go public with all he knew.

They would have killed him, just like they would have killed Nina and baby Cara still growing inside her.

"Liar," Nina hissed. "Brice would never leave me. Us."

"Believe what you want. Either way, he's dead, and so is Leon. You've made your choice, and now you're going to suffer the consequences."

"You know, I don't believe you're there."

"I'm here. What happens next is up to you," Maggie said, without missing a beat.

Tami waved her hand to tell her to keep going as she worked at top speed, the screen tracking the phone signal and bouncing across the map from country to country as it redirected through a tangled web of networks.

"If you're there, then explain to me why my mam is sitting in the kitchen having tea with the neighbor."

Maggie's heart sank.

"I have old footage on replay. Didn't want you looking in on us while I paid a visit."

Wherever Nina had planted the secret cameras in Fiona's house, Maggie hadn't spotted them. Nina may have anticipated Maggie's move, but she had the suspicion it was more to check in on how her daughter was doing. To look in on her from afar. Regardless of her reasons, Maggie's leverage had been dismantled.

"Bullshit," Nina said.

"I'm almost there," Tami whispered. "I just need a little bit longer."

"Are you really prepared to take that risk?" Maggie asked, trying to keep calm and regain control of the situation.

"Nice try, but you're going to have to be better than that. You've gotten rusty since becoming a civilian," Nina teased. "It was nice having a little catch-up, though. Did you like your surprise? I thought the roses were a nice touch."

Maggie gripped the edge of the desk so hard, it hurt. "I'm going to kill you," she promised. Promised with her entire being.

Nina laughed again. "You can try. I'll see you soon, Maggie."

Then the line went dead.

Maggie dropped the phone and it clattered on the desk.

Tami shot up from her seat. "I got it! I traced her location."

"Where is she?" Maggie asked.

"Here. In London."

Chapter 14

Nina was in the city.

Maggie collected her jacket and pocketed Fiona's phone. "Ashton, we're going to need weapons."

"One step ahead of you," Ashton said, coming out of his office and lugging a huge metallic case. He unlocked it to reveal a treasure trove of artillery. "Figured we should have some goodies kept in the office for times like these."

He toyed with some grenades but settled on an assault rifle, which was probably for the best.

"Agreed." Maggie selected a shotgun to go along with her Beretta, some extra ammunition for both, and a large hunting knife. "Tami, what's the location?"

"A self-storage facility in the Royal Docks," she replied, bringing up the map on her laptop.

Maggie studied the area and frowned. "That's five minutes from my flat."

Maggie's blood boiled at the idea of Nina being a mere stone's throw away from her. The sheer audacity to linger so close to her and Leon's home spoke of a defiant confidence that would result in Nina's downfall. They had her now, and Maggie wouldn't let her get away this time.

"I've sent the fastest route to the GPS in Ashton's car," Tami said, spinning in her chair to face them. "Estimated travel time is twenty-six minutes."

Maggie headed for the door "We need to leave now. She might already be on the move."

While Nina had caught Maggie out on her lie, the fact she'd been to her mother's and had her phone might have spooked Nina to up and leave her current location.

"Be careful, you two," Gillian called as they left. They headed to the street below where Ashton had parked his Porsche.

The sun scorched down upon them, but dark clouds circled Maggie's mind. A storm was coming, and she intended to rain down on Nina with a thunderous wrath.

"What's the plan?" Ashton asked as they got in. He pulled out onto the street and weaved through the city traffic as fast as he could. It wasn't rush hour, but each stop at a set of lights felt like eternity.

"We go in and we take her out."

Maggie had no qualms about what happened next.

She had no intentions or desire to prolong the experience, to make Nina suffer and revel in her pain before she ended her existence. Maggie wanted her dead, and the sooner the better. A swift, clean hit like she had done so many times before.

"Simple enough," Ashton said, honking the horn and yelling out his window at the driver in front of them to hurry up and move now that the light had turned green. "Bloody Sunday drivers."

"We can't let her get away."

Nina had already caused so much devastation, not only to Maggie but to the agents of the Unit who were unknowingly pimped out and used as death dealers in her and Bishop's illicit side business. To the families of the innocent people each agent had killed under one of their contracts with the very people they had sworn to stand against. To the loved ones of the agents who were exposed and killed, thanks to Nina handing over their information to Ivan Dalca's criminal syndicate.

The trail of damage went farther than any of them could comprehend, and someone needed to put a stop to it all. Nina needed to die, and Maggie would be the one to do it.

The self-storage company lay just off the docks next to Lyle Park, the surroundings sparse and industrial. Arriving at the address, Maggie checked the clock. They'd gotten there six minutes faster thanks to Ashton's driving.

"The gates are locked," he said as they approached the entrance.

A thick, rusted chain wrapped around the ten-foot gates, their iron bars blocking the way to Maggie's target.

"Drive straight through," she ordered, gripping her seat and bracing for impact.

Ashton tapped the dashboard and winced as he spoke to his car. "Sorry, baby. Needs must."

Revving the engine, Ashton slammed his foot down on the accelerator and collided into the gates. The chain broke under the impact and the gate burst open.

The car screeched to a halt, and Maggie jumped out, scanning the area for any signs of Nina. All of the facility's storage units appeared closed with their shutters down. They ran down two long rows that encompassed the plot of land, culminating in a front office on the opposite side of the gates. The empty parking lot in the middle had no signs of life anywhere.

The hair on the back of Maggie's neck stood on end at the overwhelming sense of eyes watching her. Shotgun out, Maggie motioned for Ashton to take the right side of the lockers while she headed left, checking each storage unit. All the ones she passed were sealed shut and padlocked from the outside.

Maggie eyed the ground-level office building as Ashton signaled that his row was locked too. As one, they headed toward it, veering in opposite directions. Ashton leaned against the dirty gray roughcast wall by a fire exit door and nodded at Maggie as she stole a glance through a window with slatted blinds.

The office inside was empty, desk cluttered with paper and piles of boxes off to one side. Taking the butt of her shotgun, Maggie smashed the glass with a hard thrust and attacked it until she'd made an entry point for herself.

At the other end, Ashton kicked in the door and vanished inside as Maggie hoisted herself through the window, glass crunching under her boots. Prying open the office door, she glanced out into a narrow hallway, keeping her eyes peeled for any clues of Nina's presence.

Losing patience, Maggie barged out and down the hall, kicking open every door she passed and ducking in, gun first, to examine each room before moving on to the next. A recreation room to her right looked out to the back end of the plot of land, and Maggie checked to make sure Nina hadn't slipped out the back. Nothing but dead grass and tufts of weeds stretched out beyond, the surface flat enough for Maggie to be sure Nina hadn't made a run for it.

"Clear," came Ashton's voice as Maggie made it to the end of the corridor.

"Clear," Maggie confirmed, venturing down to the middle of the building to a central foyer positioned by the empty front desk. "She's not here."

Lashing out, Maggie kicked a nearby chair and sent it

sprawling across the room, panting hard. Right on cue, Fiona's phone rang in Maggie's pocket.

Maggie answered and put the phone on speaker for Ashton to hear.

"What?" she spat.

Laughing echoed through the empty building. "Did you really think I'd be so sloppy as to lead you to my location? Pathetic."

"Hiding as usual," Maggie said, spotting the cameras tucked in the corners of the ceiling. Nina had been watching them, but from afar. "Why don't you come and face me one on one? Let's settle this and be done with it."

Nina sniggered. "One on one? Is that why you brought your little pet along?"

"Hey, Nina," Ashton said, spinning around with his middle finger up for her to see in her live feed. "Fuck you."

"So explosive," Nina replied, followed with a dramatic sigh. "Well, I'd love to stay and natter, but quite frankly, I'm bored."

Maggie pumped her shotgun and fired, aiming for the nearest camera and blowing it apart. Scattered pieces fell to the ground along with chunks of plaster from the ceiling. She moved to the next corner, and the next, not stopping until all four cameras were destroyed. She leaned down and spoke directly into the phone's speaker once she finished. "I will find you."

"You better hurry up, then. Ticktock." Without another word, Nina hung up.

Maggie screamed and launched the phone across the room. It crashed into the wall, breaking into pieces and clattering to the floor to join the remains of the obliterated cameras. They had no need for it now. With their one piece of intel compromised, all it would do is serve as a way for Nina to track them instead.

"What did she mean by ticktock?" she asked.

Ashton's eyes widened as he pointed over to the front desk. A package of some sort sat on the counter, oddly shaped and connected with an array of wires. "I think it might have something to do with that."

Maggie sucked in a breath as she spotted the timer.

A bomb.

"That bitch," Maggie sneered, running over to the bomb and examining it. Just over a minute blinked across device. "Talk to me, Ash."

Ashton knew explosives better than Maggie, having a habit of blowing things up. He studied it with a tentative glance and shook his head. "It's a good one. Nice work on her part."

"Not the point. Can you defuse it?" No one appeared to be around, but Maggie couldn't be certain. A carpet factory sat across the way, too, which appeared to be open. If the bomb had been designed with enough power, the workers inside could be caught in the radius.

The bomb beeped as if to respond and the timer went

blank. "That's not good," Ashton said, just as the device whined with a beeping sound that increased in speed.

Seeing where this was headed, Maggie grabbed her best friend and made for the door. Knowing it would be locked, Maggie fumbled with her shotgun as she ran and reloaded, a bead of sweat running down her face. She aimed at the large glass windows that framed the front wall, skipping the doors entirely.

Glass hailed down upon them. Maggie hissed as a shard sliced her cheek, but they couldn't stop.

Ashton rummaged for his car keys and unlocked the Porsche, its doors automatically opening for them. The beeping grew louder and more incessant behind them, and the next thing Maggie knew, she was being propelled through the air.

The force of the explosion sent her and Ashton sprawling as a vicious boom erupted like an angered god.

Maggie landed hard on the rough parking lot, her palms scuffing as she tried to brace herself from smacking her head. She hissed in pain, feeling tiny stones and debris dig into her exposed flesh.

Ashton got to his feet beside her and helped her up, Maggie wincing as he took her hand. Blood ran down the side of his face from a gash at his temple, but he appeared otherwise unharmed as she gave him a once-over.

The office building howled in pain as what was left of it caught fire. The remaining windows shattered under the heat and pressure as red flames licked out like demon tongues. The stench from the burning filled Maggie's lungs, and black smoke billowed into the sky in dark, ominous tendrils.

"She was one step ahead of—" Maggie began, but her words were cut short.

A second blast exploded, launching them six feet across the parking lot. Maggie landed on her back and the air evacuated her lungs with one deep gasp, winding her upon impact.

A third blast came, this time from another of the storage units, this one on the opposite side.

Clouds of dust and opaque smoke surrounded them like a war zone as storage units blew up like dominoes on each side.

"Get in the car," Maggie wheezed, trying to get up again.

"No time," Ashton said, bringing her back to her feet. Soot and grime covered his face and clothes, his immaculate hair disheveled.

Together, they surged forward as the world around them ignited.

Pieces of brick burst out toward them along with the charred contents of the units, shooting like deadly projectiles. They collided with Ashton's prized car, taking out the windshield and destroying the paint job with huge dents.

Charging past the car, Maggie and Ashton raced to stay ahead of the line of explosions, which came one after the other, bursting against Maggie's eardrums. As they neared the gate, a larger blast caught them and propelled them through the entrance to the road outside.

On the ground again, they froze and caught their breath as the destruction continued behind them, both covering their heads in fear of more to come.

Fire crackled behind them, and the eruptions finally stopped. Maggie's ears rang as she sucked in a lungful of rancid air.

Deeming it safe, she peered back to see Ashton's car up in flames with the rest of the place, his pride and joy truly beyond saving.

Her lungs burned and hair stuck to her slick forehead, the heat from the fire blistering even from their distance.

They watched the hellish destruction, both knowing they'd fallen right into Nina's trap. Maggie balled her fists, ignoring the stinging pain from her skinned palms.

Nina could be in anywhere by now, and they had no way of tracking her.

Chapter 15

Essex, United Kingdom

Maggie got out of the taxi and stared at the blue door of No. 72 Hadley Grange. She'd put it off for too long and had to face the residents inside.

She tugged at the bandages wrapped around her hands. Gillian, who happened to have first aid training among her many skills, patched her up once they returned, battered and bruised, to the Engage office.

Ashton's hit to the head had required two stitches, which he took without complaint. The cut on Maggie's cheek hadn't needed any, but it stung in painful throbs and served as a constant reminder of her failure. They were both lucky that was the extent of their injuries. Had they not acted as quick as they had, someone would be scraping pieces of them off the ground.

Maggie took a deep breath and rang the doorbell.

They didn't need to worry about Ashton's Porsche leading to questions from the police. None of his cars were actually registered to him, and the license plates were all fake. Thanks to Gillian's other skills, Ashton Price didn't exist much on paper. Not even the estate in West Sussex could be directly linked to Ashton on any official basis.

The front door opened, and unbidden tears surged as soon as Maggie laid eyes on Idris Frost.

"Who is it?" came a voice, and Sade Frost stepped into view behind her husband.

Maggie hovered at the threshold. "Sade, Idris, I'm so sorry. I should have come sooner, I just—"

Whatever she'd been about to say got lost in the deep sob that escaped her chest. Idris led Maggie inside and closed the door. They both embraced her in tight hugs, all of them clinging to each other as sorrow took over.

"I know, sweetheart. I know," Sade said in her ear, crying too.

They stood in the hall of the little suburban house and mourned the man who'd played such a huge role in all their lives. After a while, the sobs faded, and Maggie got a hold of herself.

"I'm sorry," she said again, accepting a handkerchief from Idris and wiping her face. "I'm sorry for everything."

"You have nothing to be sorry about," Sade assured, blowing her nose.

"Go and sit down, love," Idris said, his face looking drawn compared to the last time Maggie had seen him. "I'll make you both a cup of tea."

Idris ventured into the kitchen where, every fortnight, they'd gather for Sunday lunch. Idris would cook an amazing roast while Sade pretended to help and chatted away, both parents thrilled to have their boy visiting.

Maggie looked forward to these visits, not used to having a loving family, something she lacked growing up. Sade and Idris had always made her feel welcome, forever asking them both when they intended to make her an official Frost.

Sade sat next to Maggie on the couch by the window. Photos of Leon growing up lined the fireplace, from baby pictures to a family photo taken last Christmas with them all gathered by the tree. "We've been worried about you. I tried calling, but your phone was switched off."

"I didn't mean to worry you," Maggie said, wracked with guilt over not being in touch. She'd been so busy going after Nina, she'd forgotten about the other people Leon left behind. "I've just been such a mess, and I don't even know where my phone is. Everything's been a bit of a blur these past few days."

Maggie took Sade's hand in her bandaged one.

"Oh, my word, what happened to you?" Sade asked, noticing Maggie's wounds for the first time.

Maggie tried to pull her hand back. "It's nothing."

Sade frowned, concern mapping her beautiful face. "Nothing?" She cupped Maggie's jaw, careful not to go too near the cut on her cheek.

"A little car crash," Maggie assured, the lie coming easy. "Nothing to worry about."

Sade examined her with the same intense brown eyes she'd gifted Leon, kicking into nurse mode even though she'd retired from her long career at the Princess Alexandria Hospital three years ago. "Did you get checked out by a doctor?"

"Yes," Maggie lied. "I'm fine."

"Sweet lord, I couldn't bear it if anything happened to you too."

"What's that?" Idris asked, coming in with two cups of tea in hand. Maggie accepted hers but didn't drink it. She'd had enough tea to last a lifetime these past couple of days.

"Maggie was in a car crash."

"Are you okay? What happened?"

Idris mirrored Sade's concern, his features so much like Leon, it hurt to look at him. To get a glimpse at how her partner would have aged as they grew old together. Would Leon have gone plump and bald like his father, or would he have clung on to his hair, the black dusted with

139

a sprinkle of gray like his mother? Maggie would never know.

"You know London," Maggie said. "Full of crazy drivers. This guy wasn't looking where he was going and hit the car I was in. I'm fine, though, really."

"As long as you're okay," Idris said, sitting in the armchair across from them with a small groan, his knees troubling him again. "Well, as okay as can be, considering."

Maggie saw so much of Leon in his parents. In his dad's wide nose and ears that stuck out slightly. In his mother's deep eyes and full lips.

"I can't believe it," Maggie said, yet again. The shock hadn't left in the time since his death. His murder. It didn't feel real, like her mind had retreated into denial to make it easier to cope.

Idris nodded. "We've been saying the same thing."

"How can a healthy man have a heart attack out of nowhere?" Sade said, incredulous. It hadn't truly sunk in for any of them, it seemed.

They would never know the horrific truth of what had happened to their son, and while dishonest, it protected them both from hurting further. Of knowing that his time on earth had been stolen in the most dreadful fashion.

Maggie placed her tea on the coffee table, the heat painful against her tender palms. "These things happen all the time, apparently. You just never think it's going to happen to the ones you love."

"Leon's boss came around," Idris said. "Grace Helmsley. She said you found him?"

Leon's parents looked at her for answers, and Maggie chose her words very carefully.

"Yes. I came home and he was in bed. I think he passed in his sleep."

None of it was a lie. It really did appear that Leon had died at some point while he was in bed, the poison taking effect while he slept. Nina had staged the scene for Maggie, but she wouldn't have been able to move his large frame after the fact. She'd likely spiked Leon's beer or pizza and waited until he was dead before setting the trail of roses she seemed so pleased about.

"He didn't suffer, then," Sade said, more to herself than Maggie or Idris. Her shoulders relaxed, just a little.

Maggie couldn't answer that. Part of her didn't want to know the truth. Nina had a penchant for poisons that gave a slow and agonizing death. Maggie could only hope she'd chosen a fast-acting one to ensure Leon had no time to react or call for help.

Idris ran a hand over his mouth, a tremor in his fingers. "That's a small comfort at least."

"I haven't been back to the flat yet," Maggie admitted, staring down at her hands. She had no idea what state the place was in and had no plans on ever returning to find out. Her home for most of her adult life, and one that contained so many happy memories over the last year, was now condemned in her mind.

"Where are you staying?" Sade asked. "Grace said you were at a friend's? You know you can always come and stay here with us. As long as you need."

Maggie fought to control the wave of emotion at that. Leon's parents had been wonderful, treating her like part of the family since they'd met her. "Thank you, and I love you both for offering. I'm staying with Ashton for a bit until I'm ready to figure out what to do next."

"Nice lad, that boy," Idris said, both of them having met Ashton after he and Leon had rekindled their friendship.

"I'm glad he's looking after you." Sade shifted in her seat and got closer to Maggie, wrapping an arm over her shoulders. "We may have lost Leon, but we haven't lost each other. He wouldn't want that. He'd want us to stay together."

"I know." Maggie leaned into her and took comfort in her warmth. "Grace told me he'd planned a week for us in Venice."

"He did," Sade said with a sad smile. "I went with him to pick out the ring. He was so excited."

"I wish we could have ... before—"

"Me too," Idris said, clearing his throat. "I had hoped to offer to walk you down the aisle."

A tear escaped despite Maggie's best attempts to hold back her emotions. "I would have loved that, Idris."

Sade ran a hand over Maggie's head in a tender, motherly way Maggie hadn't experienced since she was a small child. "No matter what, you will always be our daughter-in-law. You hear me?"

Maggie nodded. It was all she could do at that point, unable to talk.

The doorbell rang, its chime echoing through the house.

Idris got to his feet with a groan. "I'll get it."

He exchanged a few words with someone and returned, popping his head through the living-room door.

"It's the people from the funeral home. To go over the plans for the burial. I can tell them to come around another time if it's too much for you?" he asked Maggie.

Sade straightened in her seat and turned to her. "Will you help us organize things? You were the one he loved most in the world. He'd want you to make these kinds of decisions for him."

"We'll make them together," Maggie said, squeezing Sade's hand.

Sade nodded, putting on a brave face the same way Leon did, so many of his mannerisms inherited from her. "All right, Idris, bring him in."

Maggie ran a hand through her hair and pulled herself together as the man and woman from the funeral home came in.

There was something *off* about the guy. Maggie registered it the moment they entered the room. She couldn't explain it, but experience and years of being around certain types of people had trained Maggie to look beyond the obvious.

The black, tailored suits they both wore along with their somber expressions pinned them as representatives from a funeral home. The catalogue in the man's hand had the right details on the cover, the kind that displayed all the options for coffins and flower arrangements available to mourning families.

Neither of them was overly built or imposing. Just normal people in their thirties, with dark brown hair, pale skin, and indistinct features. Too normal.

It was the way they moved that gave Maggie pause. Their footsteps barely made a sound, far too light on their feet for any normal person. As the two entered, their eyes automatically searched for exit routes and evaluated Maggie and Sade with cunning eyes that spoke volumes without them saying a word.

The eyes of killers.

In the split second it took Maggie to register all this, the woman had slipped her hand into her suit jacket and pulled out a gun.

"The Handler sends his regards."

Chapter 16

The Handler.

Maggie jumped to her feet, shoving Sade back into the couch as she got up to greet her visitors. Sade yelped in surprise, but Maggie had no time to explain.

The woman with the gun fired at Maggie, but she missed as Maggie dodged out of the way, sending a bullet into the television instead.

Lashing out with a kick, Maggie smacked the woman's hand free of her weapon. It dropped to the floor and tumbled under the couch as Maggie punch the woman as hard as she could in the solar plexus. The woman doubled over and Maggie hit her again with an uppercut, connecting with her chin and sending the hired killer back out into the hall.

As the woman fell, Maggie spun to take on the

man, heart drumming in her ears as she tried to get control of the situation. This couldn't be happening. Not here.

"Idris, don't!" she yelled, but it was too late.

Idris swung for the man, his approach desperate and unskilled. The assassin smacked Idris with an easy backhand, and he fell to the carpet.

Sade screamed and dropped from the couch, crawling over to her husband's side.

"Get out of here!" Maggie ordered as she snatched a vase from the coffee table and struck the unnamed man over the head with it. It shattered upon impact, but the killer remained standing.

"Look out!" Sade screamed.

Maggie made to move, but the woman grabbed her from behind, yanking her by the hair so she reeled backward, and punched Maggie square in the face.

Hair ripped from her scalp as Maggie twisted in the assassin's hold, getting to her knees. She swiped her arm under her opponent's legs and tripped her up, bringing her to the ground with her.

Taking a page from the woman's book, Maggie clutched her opponent's shoulder-length hair and used it to smack her head against the floor once, then twice. She made for a third time, but the man intervened.

He grabbed Maggie around the neck, the muscles in his arms and biceps deceiving in the slim-fit suit he wore. While average in height and size, he was still bigger than

Maggie, and he yanked her to her feet with ease, keeping his hold around her neck.

The woman struggled to stand, but Maggie kicked her in the face with the heel of her boot, temporarily disposing of one assassin for a few brief moments while she tried to break free from the other.

Having fought one of the Handler's men before, Maggie knew not to underestimate anyone on his payroll. One was deadly enough, and the Russian had sent two for her.

The man didn't speak, but his actions spoke volumes. He squeezed his arm, pressing down on Maggie's windpipe with unbearable pressure. Breathing was out of the question, and Maggie relaxed her body as best she could. Panicking would only kill her faster.

Retaliating with an elbow, Maggie squirmed in his hold, her attack landing but hitting hard muscle beneath his starched shirt. Wishing she'd brought a gun with her, Maggie relied on the second-best thing. A gun had felt all kinds of wrong to take with her to visit Leon's parents. They were separate from Maggie's and Leon's risky work lives, from a different world they each retreated to in order to feel normal, even if just for a lazy afternoon.

Maggie slid the knife out from its holder and wedged it into the man's side, giving the blade a vicious twist once it buried inside him.

Landing on the floor as the man let go, Maggie gasped for air, the knife still in her grip. Blood oozed from where she'd stabbed him, and the man raged. Before he could strike again, Maggie used the short distraction and rolled across the carpet, distancing herself from the woman who lunged for her. She sliced at the man in the process.

The blade's edge met skin, and Maggie swiped him across the back of both ankles, feeling the tendons sever like sliced rope.

More blood coated Sade's cream carpets as arterial spray spurted from the deep gash in each ankle. The assassin tried to stay standing, reaching out to his colleague for help, but she shoved him out of her way as she charged for Maggie.

The man crashed to the floor, hitting the wall as he fell, and Maggie braced herself. Before she could get back to her feet, the woman collided like a rugby player and tackled her with full force.

Lungs still burning, Maggie couldn't put up much of a fight. The impact sent her reeling into the coffee table behind her. The wood broke under her weight, pain shooting up her back as she landed with a hard thud.

Maggie still clutched the knife, and she slashed the blade at the woman. Missing the clumsy attack, the killer-for-hire pinned Maggie's arm to the ground.

Not letting go of her only weapon, the assassin pressed the toe of her shoe down on Maggie's already damaged hand, crushing her fingers against the blade's hilt.

Maggie roared in pain and frustration and let go of

the knife.

The assassin kicked it away, but seeing the distress it caused, she returned her boot to Maggie's hand.

"Maggie," Sade screamed, gaining the assassin's attention. Idris had managed to sit up, a droplet of blood sliding down from the corner of his busted lip, and he held a protective arm across his wife.

The pressure released on Maggie's right hand as the assassin strode over to her squirming partner and collected his gun from its holster. She turned from him and pointed the pistol at Leon's parents.

"No," Maggie groaned, rolling to her stomach and searching across the carpet. "Not them."

Recalling where the woman's gun had fallen, Maggie continued to roll across the ground to the couch. She dug underneath and her stinging hand met the cool metal of the handle.

Trained killers weren't stupid, though, and the remaining assassin caught sight of Maggie's exploits. She turned her gun on Maggie and fired, aiming true for Maggie's chest.

Idris and Sade screamed as the power from the bullet put Maggie flat on her back.

Struggling to breathe from the impact and staring up at the ceiling, Maggie ran her free hand over her T-shirt and found a bullet-shaped hole in the fabric above her heart.

The woman was a good shot.

Chapter 17

Getting shot is never fun. Even with a bulletproof vest on.

It still hurt like hell, only not as much as it could have had the assassin aimed for another, unprotected part of Maggie's body.

For her shooter's sake, Maggie played dead.

Sade's and Idris's cries assaulted her ears, more painful than any gunshot as they bore witness to her being gunned down at the hands of a ruthless intruder.

With eyes closed, Maggie listened and waited for her moment. The assassin, deeming Idris and Sade as less of a threat, crossed the room and came toward her.

Like Maggie, the woman would have been trained to shoot any targets in the head, even if they were down, to ensure no mistakes were made. That no one survived an encounter with them.

"No!" Sade screamed, informing Maggie without realizing it. Gun still in her hand, she hoisted herself up and fired three rounds while doing so. Two missed, but one imbedded into the assassin's shoulder, causing the gun to fly once more.

Had it not been for the element of surprise, her adversary would have fired first.

Undeterred from the hit, the woman pounced and landed on Maggie with her entire weight. She tried to snatch Maggie's gun, digging her nails in and dragging them across her skin like a wild animal.

Maggie held on and fired the remaining shots in her magazine into the wall and well away from Leon's parents, knowing she was moments away from her weapon being taken from her.

The shots rang through the small room with deafening ferocity before the assassin snatched the gun away. She turned it on Maggie and pulled the trigger, but no bullets shot out of the smoking barrel. Seizing the woman's collar, Maggie pulled and attacked her with a headbutt.

"You bitch," she spat in accented English, her nose bent at an angle it hadn't been seconds ago. Blood spilled freely down her mouth and chin.

Maggie's head pounded from the attack, and she blocked the flurry of blows the assassin threw her way as best she could, taking hit after hit to the kidneys and ribs as she tried to get the woman off her.

Dangerously fatigued now, Maggie stopped defending herself and stuck her thumb into the killer's shoulder where she'd shot her, resulting in a wild scream of pain. The woman reeled and Maggie moved, getting in between her and Leon's parents who watched on in astonished fear.

Even with being shot, the assassin still came at her with full force, not slowing down no matter how many times Maggie hit her.

Every part of Maggie ached as adrenaline and a deep-rooted terror for Sade and Idris sent alarm bells of panic through her and left her whole body shaking.

Knowing the odds were against her, Maggie rushed for a solution.

Glass cut into her knee as she stood, the remnants of the vase she'd cracked the man with. He still writhed in pain in the corner of the room.

A flustered Maggie hunted among the shards and found the largest piece just as the woman was on her again.

With a war cry, Maggie met the assassin in a last-ditch attempt to best her. The assassin punched her in the face, snapping Maggie's neck back. She made to kick her next, but Maggie closed the gap between them and swung her arm in the air.

The glass shard made a sickening sound as it impaled the assassin's temple. Maggie tried to pull it out, but it was lodged in tight, the protruding part cutting her hand.

She let go as the blow registered with the woman before her, shock painting her face before her eyes rolled to the back of her head and she collapsed dead onto the destroyed carpet.

Maggie rocked on her feet but steadied herself. It wasn't over.

"Look away," she told Sade and Idris.

Attempting to get one of the Handler's assassins to talk was useless. Maggie knew that from experience too. It seemed some kind of code they stuck to, either through fear of the Handler's wrath or as a display of loyalty to him.

The man clung to the backs of his ankles, trying yet failing to stanch the blood. He'd gone deathly pale, and it was only a matter of time before he joined his partner.

He swatted at Maggie as she approached, fighting till the end. She overpowered him easily enough and clamped his head between both palms. The assassin stared at her with a hollow expression and Maggie jerked her hands in a savage twist.

His neck snapped clean with a loud crack, and she let him slump into a heap.

The moment she let go, Maggie stumbled to the couch on trembling legs.

She got a fright when Sade finally spoke up.

"Maggie, what the hell is going on?"

Chapter 18

This was never a conversation Maggie planned on having, especially surrounded by the corpses of two assassins.

They must have followed her to Hadley Grange, for they were surely there for her and not Leon's parents. The fact she hadn't caught them tailing her spoke volumes to their skill. Or to Maggie's recklessness. She wasn't sure which.

Hearing the Handler's name leave the woman's lips had hit Maggie like a punch to the face. She'd met the man once, yet it was enough time for even the mention of him to put her on edge. His vow to her that day back in Moscow echoed in her mind.

You're going to regret this day. That I promise you.

It appeared he had stayed true to his word.

"Keep the ice on your lip," Sade ordered Idris. "It'll keep the swelling down."

She was the first of them both to get over the shock of what they'd witnessed. Seeing the blood and that Maggie and Idris were bleeding, she walked into the kitchen and came back with a first aid kit.

Idris sat in his armchair, ice pack in one hand, a glass of brown rum in the other. Some things even tea couldn't fix.

After making a call, Maggie allowed Sade to clean her wounds so she could assess the damage. She'd been hesitant to approach Maggie at first, which though unsurprising considering the circumstances, had stung deeper than the cuts across her hand. Seeing the uncertainty there, and the fear, made Maggie uneasy.

"Talk to me. What is going on?" Sade said, harsher than she'd ever spoken to Maggie before.

Maggie flinched. Where to begin?

She took a deep breath and uttered words that went against everything she'd been taught. After all they'd been through, they deserved the truth. At least as much as she could give them without placing them in further danger.

"Leon and I worked for the government. On things that weren't public knowledge and that we weren't allowed to talk about. Things that needed to be done to protect people but couldn't be carried out overtly by the government. Do you understand what I'm saying?"

Sade stopped cleaning Maggie's palm. "Leon was a senior manager. At the stationery company."

"That was a front," Maggie explained, testing her fingers for signs of nerve damage. "What he'd been told to tell people for their own safety, including you both. His real job was classified."

"Classified?" Idris sat forward, eyes fleeting to the dead bodies sprawled across his living-room floor. "What are you talking about?"

"It was important to keep our activities a secret. Parts of the job involved sensitive situations and information." Being vague was undoubtedly irritating, but Maggie trod through this uncharted territory carefully.

Sade returned to her work and rubbed a salve over Maggie's wounds. "And did that job include things like what you just did?"

"Yes," Maggie said, wincing at the nipping the salve caused. Though the cuts hurt and would likely leave scars, the wounds appeared superficial. She'd suffered worse.

"Like some kind of military division?" Idris asked, his leg bouncing of its own volition, an understandable nervous tic, all things considered.

Every part of her ached, and if she were to close her eyes, she'd sleep for a week. "Not exactly. Our work was more off the books."

"But how did Leon end up there? And you?" Sade asked with a tremor in her voice. "When?"

Maggie checked the time on her phone. The Unit had told her twenty minutes for first responders. Using the mirror on the wall, she peered out the window onto the street. Two men she recognized sat in a nondescript Ford out front. "I can explain everything, and I will tell you as much as I can, but right now we need to get you both to safety."

Idris put down his untouched rum and stood. "We're still in danger?"

"I believe so," Maggie said, hating herself for having inadvertently dragged them into this. "Don't worry, I'll make sure you're protected."

The Unit would see to it, for Leon's sake, if not hers.

Sade stopped wrapping the gauze around her hand. "Protected from what? Who?"

Maggie nodded toward the two assassins. "More people like them."

The Handler wouldn't give up, and there was no telling who he'd come after. The fact the assassins attacked in front of Leon's parents meant they didn't care about collateral damage, or he'd called for everyone around her to be taken out too. More would come once the Russian realized his first two soldiers had failed. Men like him didn't give up or cower away after a defeat. They doubled down and came at their enemies harder.

Idris went over to the fireplace and picked up a picture of his son as a baby, rubbing his thumb over it. "Leon didn't die of a heart attack, did he?"

"No." Maggie's face burned at admitting her participation in the lie. She waited while the truth settled in, their world upending once again in such a short period of time.

"Someone like those who attacked us killed him?" Idris asked, still staring at the framed photo in his hands.

Seeing them like this only made Maggie more determined to find Nina. To put an end to her before she could ruin another family. "Someone worse."

"Why?" Sade asked, wiping angry tears from her face. "Why would they want to hurt my son?"

A second vehicle pulled up and parked in front of the Ford, this time a black SUV with tinted windows.

"They're here," Maggie said, getting up.

Sade followed her gaze outside as the director general exited the car, accompanied by her two personal guards while a further two Unit agents began their circle around the perimeter. "What is Leon's boss doing here?"

"She's the one in charge of the department we worked for." Maggie ran a hand through her mess of a hair, unable to do much more since she was covered in dried sweat and blood. Her vest itched, but she dared not take it off when it had just saved her life.

"You keep saying *worked*," Idris noted, returning the photo with the others. "Are you not working for them anymore?"

"I left awhile ago, but Leon stayed after being

promoted," Maggie said, heading for the door. "Wait here, I'll just be a moment."

Grace stood outside waiting. She left her guards by the door and entered the Frost residence, giving Maggie a once-over. "Report."

"Two dead. The Handler sent them with his regards."

"The Handler?" Grace said, her lips thinning. "What the bloody hell does he have to do with this?" Put together as ever with a high-end power suit of royal blue and not a hair out of place in her severely cut bob, the director general crossed her arms as Maggie briefed her.

Maggie leaned against the railing of the staircase leading upstairs, not trusting herself to stand without swaying. "I think he's working with Nina again, since they both share a common enemy."

Grace noted Maggie's discomfort but didn't ask if she was okay. "You did make quite the impression on the man, from what I've been told. It seems we underestimated his threat."

While the Handler had been in cahoots with Bishop, Nina, and their associates involved in the contract ring, the criminal oligarch had merely provided his services to help them get rid of Maggie. That plan failed.

Her method of extracting the necessary information from the Russian had been effective, but it had made her an enemy who bided his time. The ramifications of the alliance between him and Nina made things so much worse than before.

"What about Leon's parents?" Grace asked.

"They're shaken but mostly unharmed." Maggie averted her eyes from her old boss. "I told them the truth."

Grace's jaw clenched and her voice rose. "You did what?"

"How else was I to explain the attack?" Maggie snapped, too tired for an argument. "I killed the assassins right in front of them."

She couldn't have very well made an excuse to cover up what happened. Maggie was a good liar, but she wasn't a magician. There'd be no pulling the wool over Idris's and Sade's eyes.

"How much did you tell them?" Grace demanded.

Maggie shrugged. "Nothing but the basics, but they deserve to know more. They need answers, Grace."

Telling them Leon died from a heart attack was bad enough. While Maggie knew it was to protect Sade and Idris just as much as it protected the Unit's secret activities, they were beyond that now. Danger had come to them, and whether Grace liked it or not, she couldn't sweep any of it under the rug.

"What you've done puts them in a precarious position."

"I'd say being attacked by two contract killers in their own home was more precarious than learning the truth of how their son died. They're not the first to know about the Unit."

Maggie avoided adding that most people who learned about the Unit often died before they could tell anyone anything. Clearance of the highest level had to be in place for anyone to know of the Unit's existence.

"No," Grace retorted, "but those who are aware are so because they need to know. We'll need to take them in."

Which had been what Maggie was hoping for. Now that they knew more than they should, both of Leon's parents had to be evaluated by the Unit and warned not to reveal what they knew to anyone. They'd put the fear of god into them to make sure neither of them said a word about any of it.

Yet it also meant they'd be under the Unit's protection, even beyond the current mess of a situation. The government kept tabs on those who knew such sensitive information, and it was in the Unit's best interest to ensure nothing bad happened to the Frosts either.

"You already have to take them in," Maggie said. "It's not safe for them here."

Grace looked over Maggie's shoulder, the male assassin's body visible from the hallway. "A valid point. We'll take them to a safe house."

Maggie sighed in relief. "Thank you."

"And what are your plans?" Grace asked.

"Same as before." The arrival of the Handler into

the fray hadn't scared Maggie off. If anything, it placed more pressure on her to put a stop to his and Nina's schemes.

"There was some commotion earlier today at the Royal Docks," Grace said, watching Maggie with those infamous scrutinizing eyes. "You wouldn't happen to know anything about it, would you?"

Maggie had no reason to lie. "A close call with Nina."

Grace's lips thinned again, a tell that would've put Maggie on edge when she was younger. "You should have made me aware."

Maggie straightened, letting go of the stair's railing. "I work for myself now. Unless you want to share information, then I advise you to stay out of my way."

Grace deflated, clearly in no mood to argue. They were on the same side after all, even if they kept their cards close. "We've had zero trace of her," Grace admitted. "A few false starts, but nothing concrete we can use. If I knew anything, I'd tell you."

Maggie swore. Some intel on Nina's whereabouts would have been nice considering she had jack on her end. She could be anywhere right now, planning her next move while they scrambled to play catch-up. Having the Handler involved only complicated things. Exponentially so.

"Well, right now we're in the same boat. Nina's prepared, and now we know she has the strength of the Handler behind her."

Grace sighed, looking her age for just the briefest of moments. "A most unfortunate alliance."

"Agreed." Maggie shuddered at the thought of two of her enemies united.

"Maggie? What's happening?" Sade asked, joining them in the hall with Idris by her side.

"Grace and her team will take you to a safe house where you'll be under their protection."

No one would know the location, not Maggie or even Grace. Only the agents chaperoning the Frosts would know, and they would stay with them until it was safe to return. It was the best Maggie could do for them, and she could only hope Nina didn't plan on using them against her like she had their son. Maggie would keep her enemy too busy for them to have time to focus on Sade and Idris.

"I'm not going anywhere until you explain to me what is going on," Sade exclaimed.

"I can't," Maggie said, wishing she could tell them everything, yet not wanting them to know anything about that part of her and Leon's life. "Not right now."

Grace stepped forward. "Mr. and Mrs. Frost, I will answer your question within reason once we reach a more secure location. I can provide ten minutes for you to pack some necessities, and then we leave."

Idris frowned, hands on Sade's shoulders. "Within reason?"

"I'll tell you anything you want to know that she doesn't answer once I return. I promise." Maggie would give them the answers they deserved, without having to sign the Official Secrets Act. Just not right now. She couldn't bear seeing the judgment in their eyes once they found out what she did. Having to kill the two assassins in front of them had been bad enough.

"Return from where?" Sade said with a spike of alarm. "You're not coming with us?"

Maggie shook her head. "I'm going to stop the people who murdered Leon."

"Maggie, please don't," Idris said, coming toward her. "We can't lose you too."

Despite all they'd witnessed, all she'd just told them, Sade and Idris pulled her into a desperate hug.

"I'm sorry, to both of you," she said, unable to explain how much their embrace meant to her, "but I have to do this."

Ten minutes later and with nothing more than a duffel bag of hastily gathered belongings, Sade and Idris were taken away in Grace's SUV. Two of the agents remained, stationed at the house in the unlikely event that Nina or the Handler's disciples made a return appearance.

They wouldn't. Maggie was sure of it.

Wherever Nina had hauled herself up, Maggie wouldn't see her again until she wanted to be found. Not that it meant Maggie didn't have plans of her own.

She might not know where Nina was, but she knew exactly where to find the Handler.

Chapter 19

Minsk, Belarus
18 June

Maggie stared out the window of the overnight train as it left the Minsk-Pasažyrski station.

She and Ashton had been traveling all day, first taking an early-morning flight to Vilnius, Lithuania, under a new set of identities courtesy of Gillian, and then driving across the border to Belarus in a rental car under a second pair of aliases. Knowing who had been watching them for what could've been months, Maggie couldn't afford to cut corners.

While a direct flight to Moscow would have gotten

them there much faster, she had no doubt the Handler had the capabilities and contacts to closely monitor who arrived in and out of the city via the airports. Trains were harder to track, and she hoped the indirect route paired with the unfamiliar names they traveled under would help conceal them until they wanted to be found.

"Not the most spacious of rooms I've had the pleasure of sleeping in," Ashton commented, almost able to touch each side of their first-class cabin with outstretched arms.

Maggie tucked her small bag away. "It'll do."

The chairs transformed into narrow twin beds, with only enough room for a tiny table wedged between where the legroom ran down the middle of the cabin. Good thing Maggie didn't suffer from claustrophobia, given the ten-hour journey ahead of them to Belorussky Station.

Kicking off her boots, Maggie plopped down on the chair and curled up. She nabbed the menu from the table and scanned the choices.

"We should have dinner delivered to the cabin," she said, her stomach rumbling. She couldn't remember the last time she'd eaten a proper meal. "I don't think it's a good idea to be seen out and about."

The train boasted a restaurant and bar, among other amenities, but anything they could do to avoid attention should be followed. She'd spotted CCTV when they boarded, and while unlikely they were being monitored by her enemies, the past few days had made Maggie paranoid. Every new face was a potential enemy, each stare from a stranger one of the Handler's assassins sizing up their target before striking with deadly intent.

After they'd ordered food and eaten their fill, they sat in their turned-down beds, wrapped in the thin white blankets as the train rumbled beyond the Belarus border into Russia. Stars blinked bright across the heavens, displayed in their full majesty through the unpolluted sky of the countryside.

Maggie worried at a loose thread on the blanket, her nails already bitten down to the quick. "We need to be careful, Ash. I was wrong to rush us into the self-storage place. We should've staked out the area first instead of barging in. Had we failed to notice the bomb, or if Nina had set it off just a few seconds before, we'd be dead right now. I'm sorry."

Ashton stretched his long legs across the small cabin, resting them at the bottom of Maggie's bed. "I ran in just as eager as you. We were both sloppy, and we let our hearts rule over of heads."

"A mistake we can't afford to repeat." They'd been so desperate to get to Nina, they'd forgotten everything they'd spoken about at the Engage meeting, about how cunning and conniving she could be. They weren't dealing with some common criminal.

In many ways, Nina played the biggest threat to Maggie compared to any job she'd taken on as an agent. Especially now with the Handler backing her up. This fight was personal for everyone involved, and stakes were too high for stupid lapses in judgment.

Grace had supplied Unit agents to guard Tami and Gillian back at Ashton's estate, which alleviated some weight off Maggie's shoulders. Knowing they'd be safe while she and Ashton hunted their adversaries gave her one less thing to worry about.

"I miss the big man already," Ashton said, turning quiet. He'd been so great during the journey there, talking the whole way about anything and everything so she didn't have to, keeping her occupied instead of allowing her to drift away into her dark thoughts.

"Leon would have hated it in here," Maggie said, spotting the tear trickle over Ashton's cheek as he stared at his fists. "His shoulders were wider than these bed frames."

A sad smile crossed Ashton's face. "He'd need to stick his feet out the window to lie down."

"Which would probably be for the best," Maggie teased, recalling Ashton mocking Leon for the smell of his boots on a mission in Baghdad. To be fair, Leon had been running for his life most of the night.

"I wished we'd all had more time. I keep thinking of the years me and him lost not speaking."

"You made up for it when you reconciled," she assured him, hating the anguish in his words.

Maggie had tried to tell herself something similar, thinking back to the years she and Leon spent being on-again, off-again, allowing their work to come first and stand in the way of their happiness. And for what? For everything they fought for to be shit on by Bishop and Nina.

They'd lost so much time together.

The last year had been everything Maggie had ever wanted and more, yet the unfairness of it all being ripped away ate at her soul.

"Sorry," Ashton said, swiping away his tears. "I shouldn't be crying to you of all people. I can't imagine how you're feeling."

"Don't ever apologize for grieving him. We all loved him, and his loss affects us all."

"We have to find her. We need to end all of this."

"We will," Maggie vowed. "I'll make her pay for what she's done if it's the last thing I do."

The Handler had to know where Nina was, or how to find her at the very least. Working so closely together would require them to keep in contact while they planned to ruin Maggie's life. Fedorov would tell Maggie everything she wanted to know.

"We'll need to find weapons once we arrive," she said.

Sneaking anything across borders on a commercial flight and train ride was a no-go. It posed too much of a risk if they got caught. Chartering a private plane like Ashton had done when Ivan Dalca attacked wasn't an option in this case. The flight records would only draw attention and were much easier to keep track of since private flights were much fewer in number coming in and out of airports.

Ekaterina Kovrova could track down the right people to get them what they needed in Moscow, her false reputation as a reclusive arms dealer being just the right alias in Maggie's roster to use. Viktor Fedorov knew that name, though, knew it was one of Maggie's, and would have used his reach as the Handler to make sure everyone in the Russian criminal underworld reported to him immediately should anyone use that name.

Ashton picked up his phone and began typing, the light from the screen illuminating his face in the dim cabin. "Leave it to me."

"Is this the same contact you used on our last visit?" Maggie asked, thinking of how they'd managed to secure a meeting with the Handler the first time around. It had required a very specific order at a bakery, an elaborate system only those deeply entrenched in Moscow's underbelly would know.

"The very one," he said, the sound of a message being sent coming from his phone.

"Can we trust them?" Maggie's circle of those she trusted didn't extend very far, and the idea of relying on someone she didn't know left her on edge.

"Aye," Ashton answered, but that was where he left it.

Maggie didn't push him on the subject. He'd always

been shifty on sharing his contacts, especially when Maggie was still an agent. Old habits die hard, and as long as this mysterious contact of his could deliver the goods, Maggie didn't care who they were. If they proved stupid enough to betray them, she'd erase their existence along with her other enemies.

"We'd better get some sleep," she said, lying down. "Tomorrow's going to be a long day."

The train was scheduled to arrive in Moscow at 2 a.m., which gave them enough time to reach their stakeout point before their target arrived at his usual destination.

They said their good-nights, and Maggie listened to the hum of the train moving across Russia until exhaustion swept her into a dreamless sleep.

Chapter 20

19 June
Moscow, Russia

The towers of the Kremlin framed the skyline along with the onion domes of Saint Basil's Cathedral as Maggie and Ashton stood waiting in an alleyway a few blocks south.

"Your contact's late," Maggie said, zipping up her leather jacket. The sun hadn't begun its ascent yet, and a chill lingered in the air.

Ashton leaned against the wall, dressed in all black like Maggie, keeping an eye out for any unwanted guests. "He'll be here."

The train had arrived at the station on schedule, but

they were cutting it close if they were to reach their next appointment. One they couldn't be late for.

Maggie checked her watch, impatience making her antsy. A rat scuttled out from a heap of rubbish stacked beside an overflowing bin and spotted them. It ran away and disappeared through a hole in the fence that blocked them from being seen by passersby.

She didn't blame the little creature. If it could sense even an ounce of the rage that filled her, Maggie would have hightailed it too.

Headlights came into view down the street and headed their way. The bright beams blinded them amid the darkness of the early morning as a sleek sports car grew closer. It pulled up at the mouth of the alley, closely followed by a black van that parked behind it.

Maggie backed away, not liking the odds. Ashton spoke of a contact, not of multiple people. The van especially gave her pause, noting the lack of windows in the back.

"Ash?"

"It's fine, Mags," he assured, walking toward the car.

The engines turned off, cutting the lights, and three men got out of the vehicles. Two from what Maggie now recognized as a red Audi R8, and the third from the ominous van. They were all Asian, and Maggie picked up a few words of Korean as they exchanged words between themselves.

"Ashton," said the driver of the R8. From the way the

other two men flanked him, Maggie pegged him as the one in charge.

Tall, with a slender frame, the man in question exuded confidence. His hair was dark and spiked, styled to frame his almost ethereal face. Add that to the expensive suit that fit him like a glove and he looked like he'd just come from a movie premiere.

He embraced Ashton with an air of familiarity and broke away with a smile tugging at his lips.

"Kang-min, good to see you," Ashton said genuinely, as opposed to the forced friendliness Maggie had witnessed him adopt when meeting other contacts. "How is business?"

"I can't complain. I was shocked to receive your message."

Ashton scratched the back of his head and gave a sheepish grin. "Sorry about the short notice."

"No worries. I'm always happy to help, you know that."

"And I appreciate it."

Maggie watched the flirt fest without comment, keen to know more about this man Ashton had never mentioned before. Neither of the other two men spoke, Maggie assuming from their large frames that they were more muscle than mouthpiece.

"Do you need anything else, other than what you requested?"

"That's more than enough. I owe you one."

Kang-min arched a perfectly sculpted eyebrow. "I'll hold you to that."

Ashton laughed. "Oh, I know you will." He turned back to Maggie and gave himself a shake. "Sorry, this is my friend, Maggie. Maggie, Kang-min."

"Mannaseo bangapseumnida," Kang-min said, paying her attention for the first time. "Nice to meet you."

"You too," Maggie replied, bemused by the little reunion playing out before her. It was difficult to tell for certain, but Maggie swore Ashton was actually blushing. His usual cocky playboy air had all but vanished in Kang-min's presence, and her curiosity burned to know more.

"Will you be in town for long?" Kang-min asked, his focus back on Ashton.

"Not if we can help it," Ashton said, sobering. "As you can imagine, we're not here for a wee week away."

Disappointment echoed through Kang-min's words. "That's too bad. I had hoped we could catch up."

"Another time," Ashton assured, his hand brushing past his admirer's.

"Of course," Kang-min said, waving toward the van. "You'll find everything you asked for inside. Given what you're about to attempt, I thought this might come in handier than one of my cars."

"Thank you. And the room?"

"All set up." Kang-min stepped closer to Ashton and handed him a set of keys.

Ashton accepted them, Kang-min's fingers lingering for longer than necessary.

"Call me when you're finished with whatever this is. It's been too long."

Kang-min rounded his two men and headed back to his car. He shot Ashton a wink before hopping into the driver's seat. The vehicle purred to life and he revved the engine before racing down the street and into the night.

"Talk about sexual tension," Maggie said. "Exactly what kind of contact is Kang-min?"

Ashton shook his head, like it wasn't important. "We have a bit of history. Nothing serious."

It never was with Ashton, but she knew him well enough to know when he wasn't telling the whole truth. With everything going on, it had been nice seeing her friend feel something other than anger and sorrow, if only for a few minutes.

"You had better take him up on his offer after this," she said. "Something tells me he'll be greatly disappointed if you don't."

"Of course, I will, did you see him? Handsome bastard." Ashton tossed the keys into the air and caught them again with a notable lift in his spirits. "Let's see what goodies he's left us, then."

He unlocked the van and headed to the back doors. They opened on well-oiled hinges to reveal the contents his mysterious contact so kindly provided.

Ashton whistled.

Maggie took in the stockpile lining the sides on installed shelves and the supplies tucked into the back. "Your man delivered."

"He didn't half," Ashton said, hopping up the step and ducking inside. "There's enough to occupy a small country here."

Any worries Maggie had about being unable to obtain weapons to protect themselves seemed silly now. There was more than either of them could carry, and Kang-min had provided ample options for any scenario they might come up against.

"Let's hope we don't need to use most of it," Maggie said, motioning for Ashton to get out. "Come on, we'd better get moving."

They closed the doors, making sure they were locked, and got into the front of the van.

"Right, off we go," Ashton said, taking the helm and turning the key in the ignition. "I don't know what it is, but I could murder a cupcake right about now."

Chapter 21

Thirty minutes after procuring their weapon-filled van, Maggie and Ashton parked down the block from the Abramov brother's bakery. The gaudy facade resembled a gingerbread house with elaborate icing framing the store's sign. In a few hours, lines of eager patrons, locals and tourists alike, would wrap around the building to get a taste of their admittedly delicious offerings.

While clearly a successful business in its own right, it also had ties to Viktor Fedorov. Yury Abramov, the grandson of one of the founding Abramov brothers, now runs the bakery as well as the shady dealings that happen behind the scenes, a legacy as old as the establishment itself.

"Déjà vu," Maggie said, noting that the shutters were still down.

Ashton turned off the engine and peered through the wing mirrors. "I can't believe it's been two years since we were last here."

So much had happened since then, yet the events and people who led them there in the first place still haunted Maggie.

"He should be here soon." Bakers rose well before the sun to start their day.

The surrounding area appeared deserted. Parked cars lined the streets, each covered with a layer of condensation that told her none of them had been used for at least a few hours. They likely belonged to the residents of the flats above the row of stores that sat shoulder to shoulder down the block.

Maggie had worried that perhaps the Handler would've stationed his assassins around the bakery in case she showed up, but only a crazy person would arrive at the doorstep of their enemies. Too bad they underestimated what their actions had driven her to.

"Hear that?" Ashton asked, lowering in the chair to mask their presence.

Maggie followed suit as the unmistakable sound of an engine grew closer. It passed them, and she caught a glimpse of a burly man riding a juiced-up motorbike. The paint job displayed a garish skull with two rolling pins as crossbones, matching the design of the helmet.

"That's our man," Maggie said. The bike looked new, but she remembered Yury from their first visit. A man like him stood out in a place that made sweet treats and delicate choux pastries.

They'd placed a tracker on Yury's car last time to hunt down the Handler, knowing their request of a meeting would result in the tattooed baker having to contact Viktor in some way. Since phones seemed to be avoided at all costs, they'd placed their bets on an old-school, face-to-face meeting. Maggie's suspicions had been correct, and they'd been able to work their way into the Handler's family home to use his wife and young daughter as leverage to force Fedorov into giving them information.

The same mistake wouldn't be made a second time, assuming they figured out how Maggie, Leon, and Ashton had managed to pull it all off. Besides, they didn't have all day to wait in the hopes that Yury may or may not go to see Viktor after closing time. More aggressive measures had to be engaged.

The shutters rattled as the baker unlocked and rolled them into themselves.

"Seems like he's opening up alone."

"Others will be arriving soon," Maggie said. "They'll need to start on today's inventory."

The shop had been filled to the max with a wide array of cakes and delicacies when Maggie went in posing as a Russian arms dealer. They sold fast, and new baked goods would need to be made fresh each day to keep up with demand.

"No time like the present, then," Ashton said, getting ready to exit.

"I'll go in," Maggie said. "You prepare the van."

With any luck, they'd be in and out before anyone saw what they were doing.

"Roger that."

Maggie slipped out of the van and closed the door as quietly as possible. Keeping close to the brick wall, she snuck down toward the bakery's entrance and risked a look inside the front window. Yury had his back to her, his long, gray hair tied in a thick braid, which, together with him wide frame and muscled arms, made him appear like a modern-day Viking.

The bell on the door chimed to announce her arrival.

"We're closed," Yury barked in Russian, calling over his shoulder as he fired up the large bread ovens behind the counter.

Maggie crossed the room, heading straight for him. "I'm not after your pastries, old man."

The man spun, and Maggie caught the glint of a huge kitchen knife in his hand. He threw it at her with such speed, she barely had time to move. The blade whizzed past with mere millimeters to spare and wedged into the wall behind her.

"You," the man snarled.

Yanking the knife free, Maggie held it in her grip and sized Yury up. "Yes, me," Maggie replied in Russian.

"Any chance you could bag me up a couple of dough-nuts? I'm starving."

Yury wasted no time and charged straight for her. While not one of the Handler's assassins, it was clear in the way he moved that the baker could handle himself. He wouldn't be taken without a fight, which was just fine with Maggie.

She tossed the blade away out of reach, afraid to hang on to it in case she lost her temper. They needed him alive.

Keeping on her toes, she waited until Yury got closer and dodged at the last moment from his reach. Momentum carried him forward and he stumbled over one of the display units, the glass cracking like spider-webs under his weight.

The man growled and came for her once more. Maggie lashed out with a kick to the stomach and sent him stumbling back. A punch to the face caught him off guard, and she used the moment to catch his braid.

Pulling it with her, Maggie jumped back and fell to the floor, landing on her stomach. The force brought the baker down with her and he landed with a loud *oomph* as the air evacuated his lungs.

Despite being winded, Yury fought on, throwing fists as Maggie climbed on top of him to pin him down. The brawler caught her in the jaw with a hard fist, but she didn't relent, using her skill to best his brawn, locking his arms in place with her legs and punching him until he stopped fighting as hard.

As the fight wore out of him, Maggie pulled out a handkerchief. Yury knew what was coming and tried to squirm under her, but it was no use. He wheezed with exertion, his face slick with sweat and the bloody nose she'd given him.

Maggie cover Yury's mouth and nose with the chloro-formed fabric and held it there until the baker stopped trying to break free.

While not the fight Maggie had been yearning, at least it had gone quickly. She got up and dusted herself off before abandoning the handkerchief and rummaging for the zip ties in her pocket.

She dipped out of the front door and gave the signal for Ashton. By the time he pulled up with the van, Maggie had Yury tied like a prized pig. They tossed him unceremoniously into the back of the van.

Ashton slammed the door closed and looked expec-tantly at Maggie. "Did you get me a cupcake?"

———

M aggie tossed the bucket of ice-cold water over their captive.
"Wake up, Yury."
The baker's eyes darted open as the water drenched

him. He'd been out for almost an hour and Maggie had grown impatient.

Yury focused on Maggie as the shock wore off, and he lunged for her. He managed about an inch forward before his confines stopped him. The rope tugged tight against his bare skin, his arms, legs, and chest secured to a metal chair with legs nailed to the ground below. The baker wasn't going anywhere.

Getting the man naked hadn't been the most pleasant experience in Maggie's life, but something about removing a prisoner's clothes shook even the toughest and most resilient of people. It made them vulnerable and exposed, which was exactly how Maggie wanted Yury.

His gaze shifted from Maggie to Ashton, who gave him a wave, and then on to the array of objects she deliberately displayed around the small room Kang-min had supplied for them. Tattered scraps of yellowed wallpaper hung off the damp bare walls, the single light bulb hanging above casting shadows of Maggie and Ashton over the Russian as they stared him down.

Metal from the various tools and torture devices glinted in the harsh light. Chains, manacles, spikes, blades, and all manner of creatively sadistic items promised that Yury was in for one hell of a time. Maggie didn't even know what some of them were, but their presence had the desired effect, and the hard-as-nails baker deflated like an undercooked sponge cake.

"I'm glad we can skip introductions and get to the point," Maggie said, snapping his attention from the horrific tools and back to her. "You know who I am, and why I'm here."

Maggie avoided speaking in Russian for Ashton's benefit and waited.

Yury sneered. "You're not long for this world," he said in heavily accented yet good English.

"Neither are you if you don't give me what I want," Maggie replied, unsurprised by the baker's initial resistance. "Where is the Handler?"

Yury laughed in some kind of attempt to intimidate her, which was difficult to achieve with his dick and balls hanging out. "Closer than you think."

Maggie walked toward the table of objects and ran her fingers over them, considering each like she was choosing a fine wine. "Good, because I'm sick of traveling. Give me his location. Now."

If Fedorov had remained in Moscow, they could reach him later that same day. Nina could be with him, too, for all Maggie knew, and the thought of the pair lingering nearby put her on edge. Anticipation stirred within her, and she had to fight to stay in control of her emotions. To not pick up the nearest sharp object and gouge it into Yury until he spilled everything he knew.

"What are you going to do? Storm into his fortress and kill him?" Yury asked, talking to her like she was a child.

"Something like that," Maggie said, her hand wrapping around her item of choice. Torture wasn't her thing, but she'd do whatever it took to find her enemies, and nothing would stand in her way.

"Foolish girl. You wouldn't get past the front door."

"That's enough chitchat," Maggie said over her shoulder. "You start talking, or I start taking fingers."

Yury's laugh rumbled in his chest, his bravado coming back the longer they spoke. "You don't scare me, whore."

Ashton made to strike the baker, but Maggie held up a hand and stopped him. Instead, she walked up to Yury and revealed the bolt cutters in her hand. The man balked, his body reacting on instinct and trying to squirm away, but there was nowhere for him to go.

Maggie smiled, and Yury Abramov screamed.

He screamed even louder when Ashton held the searing hot metal against the stub where the baker's right index finger used to be to cauterize the wound. Yury was no use to them if he bled out.

"Call me a whore again and I'll cut off something you'll miss a lot more than a finger," Maggie warned.

Yury raised his chin. He spat at her, and Maggie clipped again.

The sharpened bolt cutters sliced straight through skin, sinew, and bone like choux pastry. One simple snip, and Yury was missing another appendage.

"Look, mate, you better tell her before you start

running out of fingers. I don't know how many chocolate eclairs you're going to be able to make after this."

Ashton stopped the blood spurting from Yury's hand again with a sickening sizzle of hot metal on flesh. The stench of cooked meat permeated the room, and Maggie almost gagged. She forced the bile back down her throat, determined not to show any weakness in front of the man.

"Tell me."

Sweat dripped down Yury's face, his hands tremoring from the shock of being cut into pieces. "You don't get it, do you?" he said through chittering teeth. "British scum. No sense of loyalty."

Maggie arched an eyebrow and selected a third finger. "Let's see how loyal you are to the rest of these."

Each cut made Maggie's stomach churn. She took no pleasure from what she did, but that didn't mean she would stop, not until she got what she wanted. The sun was coming up now, and she couldn't live through another day not knowing. Of looking over her shoulder and wondering where the next attack was coming from.

The empty apartment building they had hauled up in for their little rendezvous with Yury grew haunted with the man's cries. Some pain you got used to over time. Maggie knew from experience. It appeared losing fingers wasn't one of those.

"Bitch," Yury hissed, blood coating his teeth from biting his bottom lip in an attempt to quench the agony.

Maggie shared a look with Ashton, silently questioning how far they were prepared to take things should
the Russian continue to keep his knowledge from them.
The man only had so many fingers, and despite the clear
pain he was in, they'd learned nothing.

"You're the one whining," Maggie said to their
captive. "Give me the location, and it stops."

For both their sakes, she hoped he'd do it soon. She
wasn't sure how long she could keep it up.

For the next half hour, Yury's wails echoed off the
walls, his entire body shaking uncontrollably as the
fingers lay scattered across the floor like bloody bullet
shells.

In the end, it took six fingers before Yury folded. A
seventh before he actually screamed out the location.

Maggie took the man by the chin and forced him to
look at her. "If this turns out to be a false lead, I will come
back and finish the job."

"You crazy bitch," Yury said, falling into Russian.
"You fucking piece of shit."

Maggie slapped him in the face. Hard.

"How many men will he have with him?"

Yury leaned his head back, his skin a sickly pale
tinged with green. "As many as he can get. He won't
underestimate you a second time. Viktor never enters a
war he cannot win."

"And the building itself?" Ashton asked, grimacing as
he accidentally stood on one of the removed fingers.

Yury's eyelids grew heavy and for a moment, Maggie thought he was about to throw up. "Fully guarded with the best security equipment money can buy," he said, throat dry and rough from screaming. "It's a fool's mission to try to penetrate."

"Will his family be there too?" Maggie wondered. Viktor Fedorov had a wife and daughter, Galina and little Klara. Two more innocents who didn't deserve to be wrapped up in their war. Like Fiona and Cara, Maggie wouldn't touch them. She wouldn't stoop to Nina and Viktor's level.

"No, he won't make that mistake again. He sent them off to an undisclosed location until this is over. Viktor himself doesn't even know where they are."

Smart man, Maggie thought, glad they wouldn't be with Viktor. Them getting hurt in the crossfire gave her one less thing to stress over.

"You'd better hope I make it, otherwise no one will ever find you here," Maggie warned. Kang-min knew where they were and what they were doing, but Yury didn't need to be made aware that he'd be released once it was safe. If she let him go now, he'd contact the Handler to warn him of their impending arrival. She let her meaning sink in and watched the last bit of resolve evacuate the baker's bloodshot eyes.

"I told you what you wanted to know," Yury said, slurring now. "Let me go."

Maggie patted his shoulder and headed toward the

door. "You sit tight, Yury. Make yourself comfortable while we're gone."

She hoped she'd never lay eyes on the man again, never mind have to return later to let him go. Kang-min would see to that.

"Wait," Ashton called, causing her to pause at the door. "I have another question."

"What?" Yury asked in exasperation, unable to keep focus on them as he slumped against his bounds.

"How do you make the perfect crème brûlée? Every time I try, I end up with scrambled egg."

Yury fainted in reply, and Maggie didn't blame him.

"Come on, you," she said, shepherding Ashton out of the room. "We've got planning to do."

Chapter 22

Night had fallen over Moscow, blanketing the city in shadow. They'd waited until dark to attempt their breach, much to Maggie's chagrin. Yet it was necessary, not only for the clear tactical advantages it brought but also to plan their approach. The odds of them making it out alive if they charged in blind, like they had done back in London, were slim to none.

Were this any other mission, Maggie would have avoided what they were about to do. Would have paused and held off until they could learn more and search for an alternative course of action.

Biding their time in this case could result in more death and destruction, and the Handler was their only way of finding Nina. Both had to be stopped, and one led to the other.

Sending assassins after her while she visited Leon's parents made Viktor's position clear. He wanted Maggie taken out, and he didn't care who he had to kill along the way. Eliminating him from the equation was a matter of urgency, and Maggie couldn't wait for him to bring the fight to her.

They wanted war, and she'd give it to them. They wanted blood, but it would be theirs that spilled.

Beyond, the lights from the city center blinked like clusters of stars, the night sky overcast with opaque clouds. From their position on the hillside, Maggie could see the area of downtown they'd be headed next. Yury hadn't been lying when he called the Handler's place a fortress. Six floors tall with almost an entire block to itself, Viktor Fedorov's building appeared more fitting to a high-end bank than the lair of a Mafia-style assassins' guild.

"Can you hear me?" Tami asked in Maggie's ear.

"Loud and clear," she replied, securing her earpiece.

"Good, there shouldn't be any delays in coms, even with the distance between us."

"That's comforting to know," she said, heading toward their first point of call for the evening, Ashton by her side. "We'll need your eyes and ears."

Maggie had messaged the contacts in Yury Abramov's phone once they were done with him, narrowing down those who worked in the bakery from previous messages and the employee shift patterns he kept in his calendar. A simple text to say he had some last-minute business to attend to and wouldn't be at the bakery all day had been enough to explain his absence.

None of the employees questioned him in their replies, causing Maggie to assume it wasn't out of the norm for Yury to be away carrying out work for the Handler. Regardless of what the workers thought, it was the best she could do to cover his disappearance, given the circumstances. No one had rung his phone after that, other than to leave a few messages on voicemail about orders for the bakery. Had the Handler or anyone else suspected a problem, they would have called. Or at least, Maggie hoped they would, if only to give them prior warning.

Tami spoke in her ear again. "Gillian says hi, and to please be safe."

"Tell her we'll be back at the ranch in no time," Ashton said, pulling a balaclava over his head.

"Are you at the location?"

"Almost." Maggie used the same bolt cutters from their time with Yury to break through the gates of the substation. Thankfully, electrical companies ran the mini power stations remotely these days, everything monitored from computer screens in the main power plant miles away. No personnel were on site, not even security.

"We're in."

A hum buzzed around them from the stored power, yellow signs warning of the dangers of being so close to so many volts. Maggie's skin prickled.

"Look for the power box. It should be encased in a metal frame with a locked door."

"I think I've found it," Maggie said, noting a six-foot metal container with a set of double doors in the center of the fenced enclosure. The bolt cutters broke the lock as easily as it did a handful of fingers, and the doors screeched open on whining hinges, too loud amid the constant drone of electricity.

Ashton stood near the gates, keeping watch as Maggie eyed the rows of circuit breakers inside. The substation was just outside of town, past a run-down industrial estate where most of the businesses appeared defunct. Still, given the string of bad luck they'd had, they took no chances.

"You should see a distribution board now," Tami said. "Each section covers a different sector of downtown. We need to locate the one that sends power to the Handler's building."

Cutting the power meant not only giving them a cloak of darkness under which they could enter Viktor's stronghold, but it rendered any surveillance useless. Removing those safeguards, along with Tami's ability to take out the phone lines and internet connection with her hacking expertise, gave Maggie and Ashton cover to infiltrate what Yury had admitted were highly guarded head-quarters.

The cut in electricity wouldn't go unnoticed by whoever manned the night watch, but since they weren't storming in through the front door immediately after the power dropped, Maggie banked on a suspicion being ebbed by their delayed arrival. Given the time of night, even if maintenance was sent out to the substation to investigate, it would take awhile before anyone turned up to get things running again.

Maggie turned on her flashlight and scanned the grid to match the corresponding numbers Tami read out to her. "Got it, now what?"

"Transformers like these have self-protecting fuses as backup for any electrical faults. We're going to have to disable them before we focus on the wiring."

Static turned Maggie's hair on end, and she listened on as Tami spouted a series of jargon-filled explanations that made her head hurt. She'd managed to locate the first fuse in question when Ashton came up behind her.

"What are you doing?"

"Take a few steps back," he said, rummaging through the backpack he'd brought with them from the van. Maggie aimed the flashlight at him, but he had his back to her while he tampered with the insides of the transformer.

"Ash, we need to cut the power before we can—"

"I know, I know," he said, taking her hand and

leading her toward the gates at a brisk jog. "I've got it covered."

Maggie looked back, but Ashton pulled her along until they passed the threshold of the fenced enclosure.

Explosions erupted behind them in three ear-shattering blasts. Maggie turned back to see the substation, or what remained of it, in flames. The metal box she'd been working had been reduced to nothing but fragments of metal among the dust and rubble from the upturned earth.

Electricity sparked and snapped in anger as rogue wires from the nearest transmission tower snapped and dangled in the wind.

Ahead, the lights of downtown Moscow blinked a few times before snuffing out in one fell swoop. From streetlights to the rows of windows from the skyline of buildings, the power cut and sent the area into darkness.

"Well, that's one way to do it," Maggie said, Ashton's grinning face illuminated by the flames of the decimated substation. "The power is out, Tami. Ash saw to it. We're heading to the Handler's now."

"How did he—? Never mind, I'll stay on the line while I prepare things on my end."

Maggie turned to Ashton once they got back in the van and set off. "You really need to stop looking for excuses to blow things up."

"Come on, Mags. We're spies, not electricians. Plus, this way the Handler's building isn't the only one to lose power. It'll raise less suspicion if the surrounding area experiences the same issues."

"You have a point," Maggie admitted, shaking her head. Regardless of his explosive method, phase one of their plan was complete.

Now they had to enter the belly of the beast.

Chapter 23

"Gizmo is ready for takeoff."

Gizmo, as Ashton had lovingly named it, was a state-of-the-art drone with enough bells and whistles to make Tami practically squeal with excitement once she got her digital hands on it. Controlling it from Ashton's estate back in West Sussex, Tami had spent most of the day with it scouting the Handler's hideout to gather as much intel as she could.

"Launching," Tami confirmed, and Gizmo sprang to life. Four sets of propellers buzzed like a swarm of bees and the device took off into the sky. Gusts of wind swept past, but it withstood the impact well, doing more to mask Gizmo's inevitable noise than anything else.

The Handler's building towered above them from across the street, its one-way glass windows reflecting the shadows that had descended over its part of the city. Now reaching the early hours of morning, the streets were deserted and eerily quiet in the encompassing darkness.

While a power cut may have drawn suspicion from the assassins within, it had taken Maggie and Ashton almost thirty minutes to arrive from the destroyed substation and to get ready to invade the stronghold. If Viktor and his men suspected an attack, they would have assumed it would have come as soon as the power dropped. Thanks to Ashton's forethought, the outage running as wide as it did only helped the situation appear like a technical fault more than anything else.

Maggie pulled the night-vision goggles attached to her helmet over her eyes, and the world turned green. "Ready?" she asked Ashton, decked out in the same tactical gear attire as she was. Bulletproof vest, guards covering their arms and legs, steel-toe-capped boots, the works. While sturdy enough to protect them, most of the gear was made with lightweight material and durable fibers to avoid hindering performance or getting in the way during battle.

Ashton nodded, an AR-15 slung across his back and a set of twin knives in his hands. Going in guns blazing might make an impact, but it was a surefire way to get killed quick. They needed to even the odds as much as they could before the alarm was raised and everyone inside came at them at once.

"Activating the thermal cameras," Tami confirmed.

Maggie followed the drone as it approached the

vicinity until it vanished around the corner. The wide, ostentatious windowed walls that covered the first two floors of the building allowed them to use infrared to detect body heat. While not entirely accurate, it provided them the ability to see though the glass their own vision couldn't penetrate.

Ten painstaking minutes later, the drone had finished a comprehensive circulation around the property.

"I'm picking up four bodies in the lobby, two more from the south entrance. We have a further six on the second floor, and three patrolling the grounds outside."

Fifteen against two. Not the best odds, and that wasn't including anyone else lurking around the remaining two floors above. A pit of dread seeded in Maggie's stomach, but she forced the nerves away, taking deep breaths as she fell into agent mode. They'd come this far—there was no turning back now.

Like specters, Maggie and Ashton moved in silence, keeping to the shadows as they crossed the street and approached the grounds from the east side. The goggles painted the area in shades of green, which took a little getting used to. It had been some time since Maggie had needed them for a job.

Ashton pressed himself against the brick wall and cupped his hands before him. Maggie sped up and jumped as she neared him, stepping on his hand and using him to boost over the wall. No one appeared to have spotted them yet, and Maggie pulled Ashton up and over with her, landing softly on manicured lawn. Neatly tended bushes lined the inner walls, and they used it as cover while they scanned for the three-person patrol.

"Don't underestimate the guards," Maggie whispered to her best friend. "They'll be trained assassins, like all of Handler's assets."

"Okay, I see you guys," Tami said. "Someone is approaching from your left in five, four, three ..."

Maggie leaned on the balls of her feet, unspinning the wire from her wrist. She leaped out from the bushes as the man came into view, so fast he barely had time to register her presence before she attacked.

Wrapping the garrote around his neck, Maggie pivoted behind him, held on to the handles at each side, and kicked him forward.

The wire tore through the man's skin and carotid arteries as he stumbled and Maggie pulled in the opposite direction. Spurts of blood sprayed across the white-slabbed pathway in a macabre fountain of red.

A failed scream gargled in his throat as Maggie tightened the wire, digging it deeper into his flesh to end him quick. The longer they lived, the greater the risk one of them would yell for help.

"He's down," Maggie informed Tami.

Ashton caught the guard before he collapsed and dragged him into the foliage out of the way to die alone. There wasn't much they could do about the blood, other than make sure they took down the man's other two colleagues before they spotted the undoubtable stains.

They continued down the left side of the building in silent agreement until oncoming footsteps stopped them in their tracks.

Ashton, knives at the ready, caught the woman as she rounded the corner and plunged both blades into her neck. More blood spilled, and the second guard fell like her brother-in-arms before her.

So far, so good.

"Watch out!" Tami cried.

"Zasha? You got a cigarette?"

Maggie spun before the third guard realized she wasn't the dead woman and launched herself at him. The bald man reached for his gun, but Maggie tackled him to the grass.

Abandoning her garrote, she punched the large guard in the throat as hard as she could and armed herself with a tactical knife fastened to her thigh.

Sharp stainless steel ripped him open like a teddy bear as Maggie dragged the blade up his stomach. She stabbed under his chin next, thrusting it through the skin and up into his gasping mouth, the blood spilling like green ooze in her night vision.

Blood coated her waterproof tactical wear, but she couldn't feel it. Didn't feel anything as she ended another life standing in her way. Every one of the Handler's assassins would be under orders to kill her on sight, and she met them with the same ruthlessness they'd show her.

Ending them quickly was all she could offer. She wiped the blood off her blade before returning it to her thigh.

The drone hovered thirty feet above.

"All three are down," Maggie said. At least twelve to go.

"The back entrance is still the least populated route," Tami said. "Two people are stationed near the doors. The lobby is down to three. One of them went upstairs."

"The back is it, then," Ashton said, hoisting the gutted guard up over his shoulder. "I've got an idea."

Maggie led the way as Ashton struggled with the weight of the guard, the Russian bear easily eighteen stone of pure muscle. The floor-to-ceiling windows stopped at the rear of the building, which faced away from the street with its back cordoned off from the offices behind by a high brick wall. In many ways, being in the middle of a busy city gave the Handler more cover than a secluded spot somewhere in the country. Security and CCTV from the surrounding buildings. Brightly lit streets. Plenty of witnesses. Even a police station less than a mile down the road. All stood as good deterrents.

For most people.

With the majority of those benefits eliminated, they snuck up to the back doors and placed the dead guard against it. Maggie knocked, and she and Ashton waited at either side for those inside to answer.

The door swung open, and the guard's body fell inside to audible gasps.

Someone stepped over the body and ran outside. Maggie plucked the man's pistol from his meaty hands and left Ashton to take care of him as she headed inside for the second guard.

Instead of bracing for a fight, the guard ran in the opposite direction. Maggie chased after her, refraining from using the gun. The woman spun as Maggie grew close, realizing she wouldn't make it to find backup.

A spray of bullets sunk into the floor by Maggie's feet, the gunshots echoing through the building.

"Shit, we've been compromised," she said, letting Ashton and Tami know.

With their hopes of remaining covert ruined, Maggie fired back with the stolen pistol and caught the woman in the shoulder. Another shot and she embedded a bullet into her enemy's head, taking her down on impact.

Fighting sounded behind her, and Maggie returned to Ashton outside. The remaining guard had him on the grass, throwing fists as Ashton did his best to block the blows. Maggie approached and fired at point-blank range. Brains splattered across the building wall in gory graffiti as their body count tallied to five.

Maggie held out a hand for Ashton to help him up.

"Guess they know we've crashed the party," he said, appearing unharmed from the skirmish.

"It had to happen at some point."

Inevitable, yes. Though Maggie had hoped to even the odds to a more manageable number. The element of surprise had bought their victories so far, but now an entire building of assassins knew to expect an attack.

Given that most of those stupid enough to go against the Handler didn't live long enough to bring the fight to him, it wouldn't take a genius to realize exactly who had arrived on their doorstep.

Maggie searched the sky for Gizmo, but the drone was nowhere to be found. "What's the situation in the lobby?" she asked through her earpiece.

Tami didn't respond.

"Tami?" Maggie repeated as she and Ashton ducked inside the back entrance. "Tamira, do you copy?"

"We must've gotten disconnected," Ashton whispered, ducking low with his AR-15 at the ready as they moved down a hallway that led deeper into the heart of the building.

"We can't wait around." Already the sounds of a commotion came from the front of the building and cries of alert grew nearer. Any moment now and they'd be on them.

Ashton pointed the tip of his gun toward a side door on their left. "The blueprints showed a stairwell beyond that door. Let's avoid the lobby altogether."

Creeping the rest of the distance as fast as they could without being heard, Maggie opened the door wide and Ashton headed in ready to fire. Coast clear, they marched upstairs, stopping every few seconds to listen for signs of movement. At least seven assassins had been picked up on the infrared on the second floor, each of them deadly skilled and experienced. The Handler only hired the best.

Each floor had a similar layout to the others, the previous tenants having used the place as the central offices for a high-end marketing agency. Even in the dark, it was obvious the Handler hadn't changed much, using the building as another front for his shady dealings as well as a hideout. Framed advertising posters still hung on the walls alongside corporate slogans from the previous occupants.

Skipping a run-in with the second-floor assassins, too, Maggie and Ashton took the stairs to the third level. Ashton stopped and held out a hand as a noise echoed from the next flight.

Footsteps grew nearer and Maggie dashed out, clutching her garrote. The assassin had been in a hurry, likely on his way to investigate the gunshots, but his haste cost him his life. He startled as Maggie jumped out, and she had the wire around his neck by the time he thought to grab for the sword at his waist.

Ashton kicked his grasping hand and punctured the

assassin's lungs with one of his knives, the man's last breath escaping his lips as they dumped him on the steps.

Six down, and none of them the man or woman Maggie wanted most. She picked up the dead man's sword by the hilt and weighed it in her hand. Light and well made. Balanced too. Samurai from the looks of it, though Maggie didn't know swords like she knew other weapons. Nevertheless, the shine from the polished steel spoke to her, and she held on to it as they continued to the top floor.

The fourth level posed as the most optimal location to stay away from unwanted guests. Nina and the Handler wouldn't mind allowing others to do their dirty work, leaving it to the assassins to take out intruders.

The layout they'd studied earlier that day had pointed to a large street-facing office on the fourth floor. The CEO's domain, and the place where Maggie knew she'd find her enemies. She gripped the hilt of the sword tight as they arrived at the top of the stairs and headed straight there.

A large communal lounge took up most of the top floor. The wide, open space was unpatrolled by guards, with stiff-looking sofas, vending machines, and rows of tables and chairs for workers on lunch break. They'd need to cross it to reach the CEO's office.

The pit in Maggie's stomach bloomed at the emptiness, and while most of the assassins should rightly have gone in search of the gunfire below, at least some should have remained to guard their boss.

Three hallways stretched out beyond the recreational area. Recalling the layout from the blueprints, the center hall led to their final destination.

Afraid to even whisper, Maggie and Ashton pulled out gas masks from Ashton's backpack and fixed them over their faces, repositioning the night-vision goggles to fit over them. Ashton dumped the now-empty pack and they carried on.

Maggie clung to her new sword in one hand while she opened one of the pockets of her cargo pants with the other.

They didn't wait once they arrived at the double doors to the CEO's office. Ashton kicked at the handles with his boot and the doors burst open.

Unpinning the tear-gas grenade, Maggie threw it inside and readied for whatever came out of the chemical smoke.

Static rang in Maggie's ear as she prepared for a fight, the connection to Tami coming back. "We've reached the targets," Maggie said, unsure if she'd be heard.

Seconds skipped by and no one exited the office. The gas had spread, coming out from the open doors now and engulfing them. Maggie stepped back, shoulder to shoulder with Ashton who kept his gun aimed before him.

No coughing came from beyond. No signs of life.

Something was wrong.

Maggie's stomach lurched as the time ticked by. They'd made it to the Handler's office without much difficulty. It had been relatively easy for them. Too easy.

"Tami, can you hear me?" Maggie called as the smoke billowed around them and carried on into the lounge area. "Something's not right. Can you see where the assassins are?"

"Tami can't come to the phone right now," said a voice in her ear. "Would you like to leave a message?"

Maggie's heart plummeted.

Nina.

Chapter 24

A wave of nausea crashed into Maggie that had nothing to do with the clouding tear gas.

Ashton heard the coms too and snapped his head toward Maggie, knowing what it meant.

"Oh, and by the way," Nina practically purred, "if you're looking for Viktor, he's here with me. You really have a wonderful home, Ashton."

Maggie made to speak, but the words caught in her throat as the smoke dissipated and the outline of the Handler's assassins-in-residence came into view, blocking their only exit. The smoke made it too hard to get a proper head count. Ten at least.

"If you hurt them, I'm going to—"

Nina gave a cold laugh. "What? You're all the way in Moscow on your little trespassing mission and have more than enough to deal with right now."

Tami's and Gillian's faces flashed in Maggie's mind. The very thought of Nina being in their presence filled her with debilitating fear and rage. Maggie clenched her teeth so hard, she feared the would break. "You haven't won."

"Looks like it from where I'm standing. Shame I couldn't be there to take you out myself."

"Maggie," Ashton warned as the assassins grew clearer in the weakening gas cloud. The eyes of cold-blooded killers-for-hire narrowed in on them like a pack of ravenous wolves. Whatever happened, she refused to be an easy meal.

"Goodbye, Maggie. Don't die too quick. I want you to suffer at least a little before your sorry life is ended."

As if Nina's final words were a Klaxon, the assassins charged.

Maggie brought out another canister of tear gas and launched it into the oncoming horde of killers. More smoke encompassed the hallway and ensnared everyone in a blinding mist.

Shots fired amid the confusion, and Maggie pulled Ashton to the ground with her. Still holding his gun, he aimed while on his stomach and sent a tirade of bullets into the toxic fog, crossing from left to right in the narrow confines.

Cries of pain mixed with the gunfire of multiple weapons, each blasting their own thunderous booms into the chaos. The coughing and sneezing began, the effects of the tear gas coming into play. From what Maggie spotted before throwing the gas grenade, none of their adversaries had thought to wear a mask.

And if she and Ashton made it through the next five minutes, she owed Kang-min several rounds at the nearest bar for coming through with their request.

The firing slowed and Maggie tried to decipher the calls from the assassins, but the international gang spoke too many languages, and all at once, for her to make anything out.

"They're falling back," Ashton said, getting to his feet.

Maggie followed suit, both of them clinging to the wall, inching along to avoid rogue bullets. Even with their night-vision goggles, the twosome had lost their advantage as they passed through the thick of the choking smog.

Someone ran directly into them, his face covered in white residue like a tortured ghost. A sharp sting ran up Maggie's arm as the assassin's blade nicked her in a sloppy attack. She shoved him away and returned the favor by sinking her sword into the man's gut and giving it a savage twist before sliding it back out.

The man fell to his knees, hurt though not dead, but a friendly fire shot struck him in the face, and he crumpled to the ground.

Maggie sent her final gas canister sprawling beyond to meet the retreating assassins. It hissed as it went to work, filling more of the floor with smoke, this time past the hallway and into the recreation area.

Ashton's AR-15 held forty rounds per magazine, and he let it rip into the misty void as they moved closer to the stairwell they'd snuck up in.

Tables and chairs screeched as assassins barged into them in their attempts to avoid the tear gas.

Maggie's foot hit a fallen woman holding on to her face on the floor as she choked on the fumes. She came down with the sword, forcing it through the woman's rib cage and puncturing her lungs.

More screams came as some of Ashton's blind shots hit, but each blast from the gun gave away their location. Bullets rattled into the wall behind them and ricocheted all around.

Ashton swore.

"Ash?" Maggie cried.

"I'm fine, it caught my vest," he said with a grimace, sending a flurry of shots back in the general direction of his attacker. His magazine ran out, and Maggie handed him a replacement from her cargo pants.

"Don't shoot unless you have to," she said, both hands on her sword now, stealth being their best chance to overcome the assassins in their midst.

The smoke spread over the open-plan lounge, but it thinned out in the larger space, especially near the edges of the room. Blood trickled down Maggie's arm, but she couldn't investigate the damage in favor of more immediate concerns.

Back to back with Ashton, they followed the thickest clouds of tear gas and maneuvered to the center of the room. A bullet zipped past Maggie's head, but she stayed still and listened, watching the patterns of the smoke for signs of movement.

Ashton spotted someone first and attacked, leaving Maggie alone as the grunts of a struggle turned into a woman's dying scream. The commotion bolstered some of the other assassins, and Maggie caught a glimpse of two heading her way.

A woman with cropped hair and bulging muscles reached her first with a makeshift mask covering her nose and mouth. She readied her Uzi to fire, but Maggie saw it coming and batted it away with a cutting swipe. The sword cut the woman's hands and the gun dropped, lost to the gas.

It didn't stop the attacker, however, and the female assassin threw a swing at Maggie. She dodged the first but got caught with a second. Knuckles smashed into her jaw with brute strength behind it, followed by a knee to her abdomen.

The second assassin was on her now, too, and he connected with a roundhouse kick to her head.

Before Maggie fell to the ground from the hits, the woman spun her toward the second assassin. The man was ready for her and lashed out with an uppercut to the chin that threw Maggie back three feet and onto the floor.

He was on her again as she landed, but she held on to the hilt of her sword during it all and slashed out at him with a burning fury. The blade swept across the distance between them and kissed the man's left wrist, hacking his hand clean off.

Blood spattered across Maggie's mask, hindering her vision. She struggled to her feet as the handless assassin screamed and vanished, allowing Maggie to turn her attention to the woman charging toward her again.

Still aching from the last set of blows, Maggie met her head on and swung the sword. The blade plunged into the assassin's neck with gruesome efficiency. It got stuck there, forcing Maggie to kick her away to free the weapon.

Another killer stepped out from the smoke before she could catch her breath. The slender man swiped her legs from under her with athletic speed, knocking Maggie on her arse again.

Having witnessed how sharp her stolen blade really was, she stayed on the ground and hacked at the assassin's legs. It caught him under his left knee and amputated the bottom half of his leg, coating the office carpeting in more blood.

Footsteps ran toward her and someone stumbled over her body, falling to meet her on floor. The tall woman shifted and kicked Maggie in the chest, her boots meeting

Maggie's Kevlar vest. An elbow to the stomach came next, and the glint of a stiletto peeked through from the woman's sleeve.

Maggie threw up her hands to grab the woman's arm before she brought it down on her, the tip of the hidden knife mere centimeters from Maggie's heart. Her arms shook as they struggled, the woman moving to put her weight into it. The blade was attached to a device at the woman's wrist, and all Maggie could do was hold on, her own weapon dropped to her side.

The blade moved close and Maggie tried to inch away. She dug her nails into the woman's arm, but she held on, knowing she was one last push from finishing Maggie off.

A gun sounded in the distance, and the woman fell forward over Maggie who had to pivot to barely avoid being impaled.

Ashton ran toward her, gun in hand, but someone jumped him from behind and he disappeared into the fog.

Getting up, Maggie collected her sword and went to help, her lungs burning as adrenaline surged through her body, every nerve on edge. Ashton was nowhere to be found.

She sensed someone over her shoulder, but she didn't react fast enough, and an enemy pulled up behind her. The knife slid through her tactical gear and skin as pain erupted in her back. From what she could tell, Maggie thought they'd missed one of her kidneys, but only just.

The metal left for a brief moment and before the assassin could stab again, she moved, forcing the blade to skip by her. Maggie threw her head back, her helmet smashing into the enemy's nose so hard, she heard it crack.

She disarmed the guy as he recoiled and used the distraction to toss him over her shoulder. He landed on the ground in front of her and Maggie stamped down on his neck three times until he stopped fighting back, adding a fourth nudge to be certain she'd severed his spinal cord.

A hand came down on her shoulder and Maggie spun to attack.

Ashton blocked the sword with his gun and yelled, "It's me!"

Maggie panted, taking him in. He'd lost his night vision at some point, his mask cracked across the screen. "We need to get out of here, Ash. There's too many of them."

"I've got some of those explosives left," he said, pushing Maggie out of the way and smashing the butt of his gun into the face of an approaching assassin.

Maggie darted forward and barreled into the man, both of them colliding with a woman who came from behind him. Breaking her hold on the man, Maggie spun her sword and speared it through both assassins with feral brutality.

"Blow this fucker up," Maggie said, retrieving her blade with one hand and pulling out her pistol with the other. She sent a bullet each into both assassins' heads to make sure neither followed them as she and Ashton headed for the stairwell.

"It's only enough for this part of the floor, tops."

Blood and sweat trickled over Maggie's aching body, but she prepared herself for one last push. "Then do it."

A throwing star whizzed past Ashton and lodged itself in Maggie's thigh. She yelled out in pain and anger as she yanked it out, dodging a second aimed at her face.

The culprit came into view, and Maggie snatched Ashton's gun while he readied the explosives. She let loose, shot after shot, sending an army of bullets into the assassin and those beyond who dared come close.

"Ash?" Maggie said as she let the empty magazine fall and clipped in another.

"Almost ready."

The tear gas had lost its initial potency, and Maggie eyed those left. Way more than the ten they'd originally counted. Backup must've waited in the wings from the front charge. It was now or never.

Maggie backed away, still firing, and kicked open the stairwell door. Ashton launched the explosives into the middle of the lounge, and they made their exit.

"Barricade them in," Maggie said, needing Ashton's help to push over a vending machine.

Ashton shoved her onward and down the steps. "No time," he said as the first set of explosives went off in a cataclysmic blast.

The surge blew them forward and tossed them down the stairs like rag dolls, Maggie's headgear the only thing from stopping her skull from cracking open as it smacked into the edge of the steps.

Down they fell until they crashed into each other at the foot of the third-floor staircase in a bloodied heap.

Chapter 25

Maggie vomited a mess of bile and blood. Her body shook as she retched.

The blast had wiped out the gang of assassins, along with most of the building's fourth floor. Aching and bleeding, she and Ashton descended to the ground floor and stumbled their way across the street before the police sirens and wails from the fire engines screeched through the night.

The power outage gave them ample darkness to hide in before the flashing lights came, and they managed to travel a few blocks away by the time the authorities arrived on the scene in droves.

A quick call from Ashton, and Kang-min arrived within fifteen minutes to take them to safety. Which was just as well, since Maggie couldn't have made it any further on foot.

"Take these," said the doctor in broken English. "They'll help with the pain."

Maggie accepted the pills and forced them down with some water, wincing at the acrid taste in her mouth. The meds had barely hit her stomach before she threw up again, holding onto the toilet seat to keep herself sitting up.

The doctor tutted and came back a few moments later with a filled syringe. Maggie made to protest, but he plunged the needle into her rump. "You'll feel some relief soon. Only way if you can't keep the pills down."

Maggie hardly heard him as she struggled with the numerous complaints from her body. The bathroom's tiled floor chilled her clammy skin as she sat in her underwear, too sore to even think about being self-conscious. The tactical gear sat in a messy pile in the next room, all of it needing to come off for Kang-min's on-call doctor to inspect her wounds.

"Thank you, Doctor—?"

"Park."

Maggie ducked her head to vomit again, but she had nothing left in her. The dry heaves made her eyes water. "Thank you, Dr. Park. I appreciate your help."

"It's my job," he said, before turning his attention back to Ashton in the next room.

Her new stitches already itched. The knife wound in her back and gash on her thigh promised to leave even more scars across her bruised skin. At least the strikes had missed any organs or arteries. The helmet had taken most of the damage to her head during her fall down the stairs, but according to Park, the series of blows she took from several assassins left her with a concussion.

While bone tired, that meant no sleep. Maggie couldn't relax enough to let sleep take her anyway. Not when Nina had Tami and Gillian. She and Ashton had managed to get out of the Handler's surprise welcome party alive, but the fate of their captured friends hung over Maggie with a sickening dread worse than any wound.

Certain there was no risk of being sick all over Kang-min's carpets, Maggie flushed the toilet, forced herself to her feet, and padded into the living room where Dr. Park examined Ashton.

Kang-min's swanky apartment lay in the middle of the Golden Mile, the city's most expensive and coveted residential area. Nestled between the Moscow River and Ostozhenka Street, the area was home to some of the most famous and influential people in Russia, and Maggie knew it well. She'd carried out a job a few years ago that involved breaking into the home of a government official. He'd defected but grew scared to share promised information with the British government, leaving Maggie to go and convince the man to stick to his word.

The mission had been a piece of cake compared to what they'd just been through.

"You look like shit," said her best friend. Ashton sat

on a wooden coffee table in his boxer shorts, leaning forward so the doctor could inspect a particularly nasty wound on his back. His left eye was bloodshot, and bits of dust and rubble still clung to his hair that matted together with blood.

Maggie slowly sat down on the couch and wrapped a throw over herself as her teeth began to chatter. "Not too pretty yourself right now, mate."

Ashton winced as Dr. Park cleaned the area on his back with vodka from Kang-min's bar, the poor medical practitioner having to improvise in his last-minute call-out. "I know I've had my arse kicked this bad before, I just can't remember when."

"At least we made it out alive." Maggie doubted any of the assassins did. The explosives proved stronger than even Ashton expected, and there was no walking away after being in the center of a blast that strong.

"Aye, it was a close one." He stuck a finger in his mouth and retrieved a broken veneer. Bruising blotted the side of his face, matching Maggie's, his busted lip cut and swollen.

Maggie ducked her head, too exhausted to cry and release the tsunami of emotions crashing inside her. "Too close. I'm so sorry, Ash."

"I'm just sorry the Handler and Nina weren't there."

"Do you think Tami and Gillian are—" Maggie hesitated. "Do you think they're dead?"

Ashton's face fell into a grim expression, looking as

drained as Maggie felt. "I don't know. Our only hope is that she's kept them alive as a backup plan in case their assassin ambush failed."

"It won't take long for them to hear about what happened." Even with the assassins dead, word would reach the Handler about his destroyed building. Kangmin had left with some of his men to release Yury. Since they no longer had to worry about being exposed, they no longer had use for him. They could have killed him, of course, but enough people had died and Maggie refused to risk pissing off Fedorov further. The baker was sure to inform his boss about what happened to him as soon as he called, assuming he had someone else to type in the number.

"If they suspect we made it out alive, she might use them as leverage," Ashton said as the doctor stuck a needle into his skin to begin stitching him up. "As bait."

"You think?" Maggie said, desperate for it to be true.

Ashton shrugged, earning him a slap on the head and a stern word from the doctor not to move. "It's what I'd do in her situation," he continued, "and from what we know of Nina, she's not beyond using innocent people in her twisted games."

"I hope you're right." Regardless of whatever plans Nina may have for them, if Ashton's hunch proved true, Tami and Gillian might not be gone yet. Maggie clung to that shred of hope.

But even if their friends were alive, for now, others most certainly were not.

The Unit agents Grace sent to protect Tami and Gillian while they were away would be dead. No doubt about that. Or the fact that Nina would have taken great pleasure in seeing her former colleagues die. She'd attempted to wipe them all out once before. Maggie didn't know the exact number on guard duty at Ashton's estate, but Nina and the Handler wouldn't have spared a single one of them in their ambush.

Maggie pulled the throw tighter. Those agents were dead because of her. Leon, too. Not by her hand, but because Nina wanted to hurt her. To make her suffer before they took her out. Killing Maggie wasn't enough for Nina.

Dr. Park inserted a set of tongs into a wound in Ashton's shoulder and her friend bit into a piece of fabric, screaming through it as the doctor searched for the bullet inside. He found it on the second try and pulled the metal out. It clattered on the coffee table as blood trickled across Ashton's chest, and his face turned sickly pale.

Ashton could have died back in that building. They'd made it out by the skin of their teeth. How many times was she willing to let him follow her into danger? To allow him to take bullets that were meant for her?

Being associated with Maggie put everyone around her at risk. They paid the price for a deadly feud that she could have stopped two years ago back in St. Paul's

Cathedral. If only she'd been as cold as Nina and handed her over to the Unit. Or killed her on the spot. Had Maggie done so, none of this would have happened.

"Should we call Grace?" Ashton asked.

Maggie shook her head. "The agents will have had to check in with Unit HQ every hour. She'll know by now that something's up."

It wouldn't take a rocket scientist to figure out what a drop in coms meant, or who would've been behind it.

Just then, the door to the apartment opened. Maggie sprang to her feet, snatching the pistol she'd left on the coffee table, and aimed it at the men who walked inside.

Kang-min didn't so much as blink at having a gun pointed at him, and nodded for his entourage of three to stop as they reached for their own weapons.

"Sorry," Maggie said, shoulders relaxing.

"No worries." Kang-min crossed the room to Ashton's side, appearing more pristine than ever in his expensive suit next to her dirty and bloodied-up friend. "How are you feeling?"

Ashton groaned as he endured even more stitches from the doctor. "Like I've been shot and stabbed."

Kang-min and Dr. Park exchanged a few words in Korean. Though Maggie didn't speak the language, the worry in Kang-min's face lessened and was replaced with clear relief.

"You need to take it easy," he told Ashton, "But you should make a full recovery in time."

Maggie relaxed a little at the news herself. The bullet hole in Ashton's shoulder had a nasty redness to it, but at least it would cause no apparent lasting damage.

"Better keep your hands off me then," Ashton said, managing a signature grin at his so-called-friend. "I need my rest."

Kang-min caressed Ashton's face with a gentle hand. "You're worth the wait."

Maggie gathered the throw and wrapped it around her shoulders, only now realizing she stood almost naked in a room with six men. She got the impression most of them didn't notice or care, and awkwardly slipped past Kang-min as he and Ashton shared a moment.

"I'm going to go lie down for a bit."

"No sleeping," Dr. Park ordered, taking off his gloves.

"I won't," she promised. "My head is killing me and I just need a dark room to sit in until those drugs of yours kick in."

Kang-min pulled away from Ashton for a moment and gestured down the hall. "Second door to your right. I had your things from the van left in there for you. Let me know if you need anything."

"Thank you," Maggie said. "For everything."

Without him, she and Ashton would have been in a right mess. They owed him, big time.

Kang-min nodded. "Any friend of Ashton's is a friend of mine."

"Likewise," Maggie said with a small smile and left the boys to it.

She closed the door behind her and entered a bedroom. The small bag of belongings she had for the trip sat on a chaise lounge at the foot of a queen-sized bed. Fresh towels and a robe had been left out for her, and Maggie replaced the throw with the soft cotton.

Careful of her stitches, she sat down on the bed as a dark numbness overcame her. Light from outside pooled into the room, illuminating everything it touched in a gloomy blue while the impact from all that had happened forced its way into Maggie's mind now she had nothing to distract her.

Dr. Park had no need to worry about her falling asleep. Her mind reeled with an overwhelming sense of both urgency and utter dread. Had she anything left in her stomach, she'd be back in the bathroom at the thought of her friends being in Nina's clutches.

There was no telling what had happened to them yet, or what Nina had planned. They must be terrified, and Maggie wasn't there to assure them everything would be okay. Even if she could, it would be a lie. Things were far from it.

Poor Tami had already been through so much, had suffered more than anyone should have to in a lifetime, and she was still so young. Things had just been settling down for her. Tami had worked so hard to build a new life for herself, and now thanks to Maggie, she was caught in the throes of a situation that had nothing to do with her.

Gillian had a husband and two children at home. She'd been so careful in her years as a forger not to get involved in any life-threatening situations, but within a few days working at Engage, her life was at risk. She and Tami could already be dead, and their deaths would be on Maggie. This was her fight, and she'd dragged them into it by letting them help her. She should have handled Nina alone and escaped Ashton when he came chasing after her in Ireland.

She could have done it. Easily. What happened to Leon should have made it clear she couldn't involve anyone else she loved, but she'd ignored that. It was selfish of her, and she hated herself for being so weak. Ashton was down the hall with a bullet wound. Had the assassin's aim been better, that same bullet could have been the end of him.

Leon. Her mother. Even bloody Bishop. They were all gone. Everything Maggie touched turned to ash. Like death followed her around as a silent companion and infected those stupid enough to let her into their lives. All of this was because of her, yet she was the one who still lived.

Maggie stared at the gun in her hand, just realizing she'd brought it with her. She could pull the trigger. Blow her brains out there and then and it would all be over. Nina wouldn't have the satisfaction of killing her, and the nightmare Maggie had been living in would end.

Removing herself from the equation left Nina with no use for Tami and Gillian. She couldn't use them against her and might let both of them live.

One shot. That's all it would take. She'd witnessed, and been on the giving end, of enough head shots to know that death would be swift. A split second.

Maggie had spent most of her life killing others. Had expected her own death more times than she could count while out in the field.

Even with her hands shaking as they were, it was one shot she wouldn't miss. The easiest target in her career. She could do it.

Maggie didn't know how long she sat there contemplating ending it all, but eventually she put the gun down on the bedside dresser.

She knew the truth of the matter. Nina wouldn't let Tami and Gillian go. If anything, she'd take her frustrations out on them if Maggie chose to exit by her own hand. Leaving now wasn't an option, no matter how tempting or easy it would be. Her friends needed her.

For Nina to let them go, she'd have to come up with something good. Something that would make sure no harm came to them, or Ashton. She couldn't bear the thought of it, and Maggie was prepared to do anything to protect them. No matter the cost.

Thankfully for Maggie, she knew exactly what would make Nina give them up.

An exchange.

Taking Yury's phone from her backpack, Maggie rang Ashton's house phone number at the estate and waited.

"Price residence," answered a voice Maggie knew.

"Put Nina on, you bastard," she spat. Her time with the Handler would come, but Nina was the one in charge.

The Russian laughed and his accomplice came on the line a few moments later.

"Still alive then," Nina said. "How unfortunate. I'll make sure you're not around for much longer. Promise."

Maggie bit her tongue to avoid antagonizing her enemy. "Are they still alive?"

"For now."

Maggie forced back a cry of relief and pulled herself together as a tiny fragment of hope emerged. Tami and Gillian were alive, and as long as they were, Maggie would fight for them to her dying breath. Even if it meant sacrificing herself to ensure they lived.

"Then I propose a trade. It's me you want."

"You'd give yourself up for them?" Nina sounded surprised, but of course she would. Acts of selflessness must have been such a foreign concept for a narcissist like her to try and grasp.

"Yes," Maggie said, needing no time to think on it.

"Then let's talk."

Chapter 26

20 June
West Sussex, Great Britain

Maggie walked through the gates of Ashton's estate alone.

Security cameras turned to face her as she crossed the threshold into enemy territory. The late-afternoon sun shone across the paved road leading up to the house, though Maggie felt less than welcome. It had only been eight days since the members of Engage enjoyed their little celebration inside, though it could have been a lifetime ago. In many ways, it was.

Travelling back from Moscow had been agonizing as

the hours stretched on and trepidation for what was to come grew inside Maggie like a malignant tumor.

It had been a simple solution in the end. Nina had no true interest in Tami and Gillian, or even Ashton for that matter. They were simply pawns in Nina's games, and Maggie had no interest in playing anymore. It ended tonight, and those she cared for most, those who were left, would be safe.

At every stage, Nina had outsmarted and outmaneuvered Maggie, relishing in her futile attempts to reach her. Nina managed to stay one step ahead, no matter how close she got. Now here Maggie was, willingly surrendering and handing herself over to the woman who ruined everything.

Nothing had changed her mind on the way there, but still sweat formed under her armpits as deep-seated nerves ate into her resolve. Whatever Nina had planned for her, Maggie knew her old friend would drag it out, making her revenge last as long as she could before finally ending Maggie's life. Nina had planned everything for so long that a simple bullet at point-blank range wouldn't be enough to satisfy her, and she was nothing if not inventive when it came to murder.

Maggie had never taken pleasure in killing, making each hit as quick and efficient as possible. The same had never been true of Nina.

Run-down and exhausted after everything she'd gone through over the last week, Maggie kept her shoulders back and head held high as she drew closer to the house, conscious of the eyes on her, even if she couldn't see them all.

The scope of a sniper rifle glinted from the rooftop of the gun range, with another assassin on the gym's roof, both of their weapons trained on her and ready to fire should their boss give the order. Maggie wasn't stupid enough to try anything under their careful watch.

Two more conspicuous sentries stationed by the front doors met her with barely-contained contempt. It seemed the man and woman weren't too happy that she'd blown up what she assumed to be the majority of the Handler's roster of contract killers.

"Sorry about your comrades," she said, as the woman searched her with rough hands. Maggie bit the inside of her cheek and kept her face impassive as the pat down reached the knife wound in her back. It stung like a bitch and Maggie had to fight the urge to smack the assassin.

Before leaving Kang-min's apartment, she'd nabbed pain relief from Dr. Park's medical bag, and while the pills were stronger than anything over the counter, the injuries she'd sustained the night before continued to make their presence known.

Every part of her hurt, her pale skin marred with a myriad of cuts, scrapes, and bruises of various sizes and colors. The side of her face had swollen during the few hours of fitful sleep she caught on the plane after it became clear her concussion wasn't as serious as it could have been. Makeup couldn't cover it, so she chose not to bother attempting to mask the damage she'd taken.

Satisfied Maggie had no concealed weapons on her, the guards opened the front doors and shoved her in front of them. They led the way through Ashton's commandeered home like they owned the place, their blasé attitude prickling Maggie's already short temper.

Blood stained the floors in the hallway, the walls peppered with bullet holes. The Unit agents hadn't gone down without a fight, and Maggie hoped they'd managed to at least take some of the Handler's assassins with them before they fell.

Each of them represented one more wasted life needlessly taken in Nina's crusade against her. One more life on Maggie's conscience.

They passed more grim-faced cutthroats on the way, heading upstairs and through a set of double doors into Ashton's sprawling office.

Two armed assassins edged around the room, covering the exits as her escorts closed the doors and shoved her into the middle of the room.

Bookshelves lined the walls with a collection that would put any library to shame, ranging from historic texts to the latest bestsellers that she'd spent many a lazy Sunday perusing. Large windows overlooked the surrounding grounds behind a large maple desk, the incoming light illuminating more blood spattered across paper spines.

Maggie's fingers tremored as she laid eyes on two figures with their backs to her, both peering out into Ashton's gardens like lord and lady of the manor. Nails dug into her palms as a storm brewed inside of her, begging to be released. To unleash its wrath on everyone around her with a swift and wild fury.

"Ah, our guest has arrived," said the man, turning to face Maggie.

The Handler snarled a grin at her, those harsh green eyes of his piercing right through her like a knife. He hadn't changed much since she'd last met him. Salt and pepper hair still slicked back with too much gel. Clean shaven with a strong jaw. A toned and muscular physique impressive for his age.

His domineering presence and predatory demeanor still gave her chills, but she didn't care about him. The Handler may have played his role in upending Maggie's life, but neither he nor his assassins had been the one to murder her lover.

"Hello, Maggie," said the woman, and Maggie came face-to-face with Leon's killer.

"Nina."

Chapter 27

Nina eyed Maggie up and down and took in the evidence of the arse-kicking she'd received as a result of her and the Handler's trap. "Look at the state of you."

"You should see the other guys." Maggie eyed Viktor and switched to Russian. "You'll be scraping your assassins off the walls and floors of your building for weeks. What's left of it, anyway."

Viktor's eye twitched, the only sign of anger in his otherwise-cool demeanor. "My hand is far reaching, and like the hydra, when you take down one of my assassins, two more will come for you in their stead. They will keep coming until you are eliminated."

"Not that they need to hunt for you now," Nina interjected, as fluent in Russian as Maggie.

Memories of them eating chocolate together in their

room at Westbrook and complaining about their strict language teacher flashed in Maggie's mind. So much had changed since then.

She took a step toward Nina, but the large hand of the guard who escorted her there landed on her shoulder. "All of this could have been avoided if you'd come for me directly."

Nina laughed like the thought had never occurred to her. "And where would the fun in that be?"

Maggie swiped the guard's hand off but stood her ground. She'd have half a magazine of bullets in her before she made it halfway to Nina. Every person in the room wanted her dead and each would gladly be the one to kill her.

"Fun? Is this all some kind of a game to you?"

Any vindictive humor vanished from Nina's beautiful face. "Far from it. This is good old-fashioned revenge."

"Things didn't need to happen this way."

"I'm quite happy with how it turned out myself."

"You have a daughter at home, waiting on you. I gave you a second chance and you threw it in my face. You could be with little Cara right now, being the mother she needs and filling her life with love, yet here you are causing even more pain and death."

Instead of vanishing somewhere safe to raise her and Bishop's daughter, Nina had spent the time since their last run-in planning the ruin of Maggie's life. In that, at least, her old friend had succeeded.

Nina's eyes bore into her from across the large office. "Hurts, doesn't it? Having the one you love most ripped away from you."

Ten steps and she'd reach her. Ten steps to wrap her hands around her throat and never let go, even as the others shot her. She could take Nina with her. Make sure of it.

Every part of her craved to do it, so tempted to charge at her enemy there and then that Maggie had to consciously focus on keeping her feet rooted to the ground. Tami and Gillian's lives depended on it, and she couldn't risk losing them to her own desperate need for retribution.

"More than anything," Maggie admitted, voice breaking despite her efforts. "Though at least Leon loved me just as much as I loved him."

Undeniable love like that was once in a lifetime, and Nina had ripped it away from Maggie like it was nothing. The vacant hole where her heart used to be physically ached for Leon, desperately wishing he could be there with her. To stand against her enemies like he'd done countless times before. With Leon by her side, Maggie could do anything. With him gone, she'd lost part of herself. The part that held the inner strength to get through anything. The part that knew, no matter what, that he'd be there. She was alone now, and that was the way it had to be to save her friends.

"Brice loved me," Nina snapped.

Even in her anger, Nina didn't draw nearer to Maggie. Like she could sense the feral nature of her rage and didn't dare get too close. Nina was many things, but no one could ever accuse her of being dumb. Unable to get her hands on her, Maggie resorted to hurting her in other ways, and started with some home truths.

"Bishop loved himself more than anyone. Then his daughters. I think he even still loved his ex-wife, June, despite all they'd been through. But not you. You were a mistake. He only kept you around because he was lonely. He admitted that to me right before he died."

"Before you killed him." Nina slammed her fist down on Ashton's desk, then sent the contents crashing to the floor. The computer monitor cracked as piles of paper fluttered to the ground and landed over the mess of office supplies.

The Handler and his team remained silent and watched, none of them taking their attention away from Maggie. Each knew how much of a danger she posed, even surrounded, with no weapons of her own. The tension between her and Nina grew palpable, like static electricity in the air. A ticking time bomb ready to explode.

"Before he took the coward's way out and tossed

himself off the cathedral roof," Maggie yelled, any semblance of patience lost. "I've told you this already."

"That's bullshit!" Nina shook her head, but Maggie could see the doubt behind her eyes.

"Why wouldn't I admit to killing him if I did? Think about it. If anything, the Unit would have rewarded me for taking him out. He knew his future was short once I discovered the truth, so he decided to end things early before the Unit got to him."

The summer sun shone through the large windows behind Nina, her frame blocking most of the light like a black hole.

"By your hand or not, Brice died because of you."

"He framed me for murder to keep his side business under wraps. He died because he underestimated me."

Even if Maggie hadn't gotten too close to unveiling the truth for him to feel the need to set her up, it would have been a matter of time before it all came out. The pressure and stress from what he had been doing had whittled away at Bishop. It made him desperate, and desperate people made mistakes. A slipup was unavoidable and inevitable. All Maggie did was speed things up by being good at her job.

"You're lying," Nina said, still keeping her distance from Maggie. "Everything that comes out of your bitch mouth is a lie. Bishop loved me. We loved each other more than anything in the world."

Maggie gave Nina a sad smile. Not because she felt

sorry for the woman, but because she knew how much it would enrage her further. Call it petty, but Maggie reveled in any pain or suffering she could cause Nina. She deserved it, and so much more.

"I don't doubt you felt that way. Brice Bishop was the best liar I knew, and you fell for those lies just as much as the rest of us. More so, actually. He played you. Once you discovered he was hiring us all out for contract hits, he only kept you around to avoid being exposed."

"No."

"Yes, and that makes you just as bad as Bishop. Maybe even worse. He did what he did because he was desperate. June had him in a vicious custody battle for his kids and that along with his secret gambling habit drained him dry. He needed money and chose a disgusting route to get it. You simply helped him out because you had a thing for him. You both went against everything being an agent stood for and screwed over the rest of us like it was nothing. You betrayed us all."

"Open your eyes, Maggie," Nina snapped, crossing her arms. "You act all high and mighty like you have some moral high ground, but in the end, you're a killer, just like the rest of us."

Maggie glared at Nina. "I'm nothing like you."

She took in all of the others in the room, each having killed for nothing more than cold hard cash. Maggie was nothing like any of them.

Yet even so, Nina's words cut deep, weaving their

way into the struggles she'd been dealing with in trying to come to terms with what Bishop had her do under the pretense of Unit missions.

Nina caught her discomfort and pounced on it. "Bishop had you carry out more of his jobs than any of us. He always sent you when he could because you'd get the job done. You acted superior to everyone else, but being Bishop's favorite made you the worst agent of us all. You murdered more so-called innocents than anyone at the Unit, and willingly followed Brice without question."

"I didn't know," Maggie said in barely a whisper.

Leon had offered to tell her about the fake missions she'd been sent on, but she didn't want to learn anything about them. Didn't want to be able to put names and faces to the destruction she'd caused. To know the impact her actions had had on the lives of the families and loved ones her targets had left behind, or how the criminals who contracted the killings benefited from taking her victims out of the equation.

She knew one name—Adam Richmond, the investigative reporter whose neck she snapped on a yacht in Cannes. He'd been working on exposing the mayor of London for his horrific housing scheme, which involved the killing of an old man who refused to move out of his lifelong home so a private company in cahoots with the mayor could erect a shopping center.

Adam had been a good man, trying to change the world and do the right thing, and she'd murdered him thinking she was doing the same. It had haunted her ever since, and Maggie couldn't live with knowing the full extent of her actions. Of knowing the names and lives of the others in her extensive death toll.

"Like any of it matters," Nina said, as if it was nothing. "Do you think everyone the Unit had you take out on official jobs were evil villains for you to stop? Did you believe you were some kind of hero? The government had you remove people who got in their way, simple as that. The world isn't this black and white place you desperately try to believe it is. You were a hired assassin working for the benefit of others. That's no different from what Viktor here does, or what Bishop did, so save your little speech on morality."

Fedorov winked at Maggie and her skin crawled.

There was a big difference, but Nina would never see it. Whether she'd actually convinced herself to believe they were the same, or she simply told herself that to be able to sleep at night, Maggie didn't care.

"Enough talking," she said. "We had a deal."

"That we did." Nina snapped her fingers at one of the assassins by the side door. The man slinked out of the room and returned a few moments later with Tami and Gillian.

"Maggie!" Tami cried as the assassin shoved her to her knees with Gillian in the corner of the room next to the towering bookshelves.

Their hands were bound, clothes stained with blood she hoped wasn't their own.

Maggie ignored Nina and ran over to them. "Are you both okay?" she asked, starting to free them from the rope restraints.

Seeing them filled Maggie with conflicting emotions. While overjoyed they were alive, the women hadn't gone down without a fight, as evident from their cuts and bruises. Neither of them had stood a chance against a team of assassins, and beating them like this had been a liberty. One that Maggie wished to pay back tenfold on each and every one of the men and women who dared lay a finger on her dear friends.

"We're fine, love," Gillian said, sporting a black eye. "What are you doing here?"

"I'm getting you both out of here," Maggie said. The rope had cut into the skin at their wrists, tied far tighter than necessary.

"Where's Ashton?" Tami asked, her bottom lip cut and swollen. "Is he okay?"

"He doesn't know I'm here," Maggie said, loud enough for the entire room to hear. "He'd only try to stop me."

"From what?" Gillian said, frowning as she flexed her fingers now that her hands were free.

"It's me they want," Maggie said, moving on to Tami and avoiding each of their stares. "This is my mess, and you'll be safe now."

Nina cleared her throat. "Yeah, about that."

"What?" Maggie spat, turning to her, not liking the change in her tone. The cocky assuredness was back, paired with a smug face that needed a good punching.

Nina checked her nails, reveling in the wave of apprehension that must have been plain on Maggie's face. Tami gripped Maggie's hand, squeezing it in assurance that everything was okay, even though she knew things were far from it.

"I know we'd come to an agreement," Nina said, "but I'm afraid I've changed my mind."

Maggie got to her feet and balled her fists so hard her knuckles cracked. "We had a deal."

The Handler laughed from behind Nina.

"Come on, Maggie," Nina said, talking to her like she was a dense little schoolgirl. "Deals are based on leverage. You had something I wanted, while I had something you wanted. Now that you're here, I have what I want, so why would I give up these two when I don't have to?"

Tami and Gillian looked on, realization crossing their faces at what Maggie had planned to exchange for their freedom. "Oh, Maggie, love," Gillian said, tears slipping down her plump cheeks.

Maggie made for Nina, but the two guards who'd brought her to the office held her back. "Even countries at war follow a just conduct of rules. You gave me your word."

"We're not at war anymore. In case you haven't

noticed, I've won." Nina's brow furrowed and she appeared genuinely perplexed at Maggie's naivete. "You didn't really think I'd let them go, did you?"

Shadows stretched out from behind Nina across the sun-lit carpet as figures came into view from outside the windows of Ashton's office.

"No." Maggie shot Nina a satisfied smirk. "But did you really think I'd come here alone?"

Chapter 28

Glass shattered as the cavalry smashed through the windows, hanging from cords attached to the roof of the house. The well-trained detail was clad in black tactical gear like Maggie and Ashton had worn back in Russia, each of them armed to the teeth, invading the office like specters of malevolent shadow.

"No," Nina screamed as chaos erupted.

Maggie spun on the two guards flanking her, making the most of the distraction. The woman sucked in a gasping breath of air as Maggie punched her in the throat. The man made to grab her, but Maggie kicked him in the stomach and sent him back three paces.

Closing the gap, Maggie lunged and clipped him on the chin with an uppercut that brought him to the ground. She made to attack him again, to ensure he wouldn't get back up, but someone charged into the side of her in a rugby tackle and toppled her to the floor.

The assassin who had fetched Tami and Gillian said something in what she thought was Greek before pulling out a knife and aiming it at her eyes. Maggie moved in the nick to time, his blade grazing the side of her cheek instead, sinking into the thick carpet below.

Maggie brought her knee to the man's groin as hard as she could, then grabbed him by his shirt collar, headbutting him before the pain even had a chance to register in his lower regions.

Shoving him off, Maggie scrambled to her feet and scanned the room.

Assassins spilled into the office as the main doors burst open. Grunts, gun fire, blows, and screaming joined together in an orchestra of pandemonium as the Unit's finest battled with the enemy.

Bullets whipped through the air from outside into the room as the snipers joined the fray. One caught a Unit agent and the impact from the huge bullets sent him sprawling through the air and crashing into the bookshelves.

Maggie clutched the blade she'd narrowly avoided next to the squirming assassin and returned the favor to him. Only she didn't miss. Blood coated her hands as she yanked the knife out of the man's chest, but she didn't hang around to watch him die.

The room had filled with bodies and Maggie searched through them for Nina.

She caught a glimpse of her brown hair amid the fighting and headed that way, pushing assassins out of her path and dispatching anyone stupid enough to try and delay her.

A scream rang out behind her and Maggie spotted an assassin cornering Tami and Gillian. Gillian stood in front of Tami, protecting her with motherly instinct, but the assassin backhanded her across the jaw and raised his shotgun.

Maggie was moving before she even realized it, abandoning her direct route to Nina. She roared and sank the knife into the assassin's back, over and over again, blood splattering across her face. No one was taking another person she loved from her. Ever again.

"Maggie, he's dead. He's dead, love."

Gillian placed her hand on Maggie's back and took the knife from her as she breathed in heavy gulps of air. She gave herself a shake, coming out of the red mist that had come over her to see the massacred assassin lying in a bloody heap at their feet.

"Take this, and get out of here," Maggie said, handing the shotgun over to Gillian. The assassin had a holster on his hip, and she found a pistol which she placed in Tami's trembling hands.

"I'm better with a knife," Gillian said, keeping the blade instead and returning the shotgun to Maggie. She nodded, having no time to argue over the benefits of a shotgun compared to a hunting blade.

Someone came toward them, and Maggie fired, blasting a hole through the woman's stomach and freeing a way out for her friends.

"Where's Ashton?" Tami asked, holding back.

"He's okay. He's here," Maggie said, leading her out behind Gillian. "Now go."

Maggie returned to the stabbed assassin for ammo. He had a belt for the bullets, and she maneuvered it off his corpse and put it on over her shoulder before diving back into the fold.

A sniper's bullet whipped past her and slammed into the bookshelf behind her with a loud *thunk*. A second one came, this time ripping right through a Unit agent's chest.

Making her way toward the shattered windows, Maggie eyed an assassin with a scoped assault rifle, shooting at a Unit agent who dived behind the mahogany desk. "Hey you," Maggie called.

The assassin spun at her voice and Maggie fired before the woman had time react. The impact sent her flying back, and Maggie collected the rifle with her free hand.

A head popped up from behind the desk. "Mags, fancy meeting you here."

"Still alive, I see."

"Barely," Ashton said, kicking the dead assassin as he

passed her body. "That one tried to turn me into a colander."

"Hold this, will you?" Maggie asked, passing him the shotgun.

Ashton took hold of it and spun it on Maggie, but before she had time to wonder what was happening, he fired over her shoulder and blasted an assassin sneaking up behind her.

"Thanks," Maggie said, using Ashton's desk as cover and aiming outside with the assault rifle. She didn't bother searching around the grounds through the scope. She knew exactly where the shooter hid.

Right where she last saw him on the way in, the sniper peered through his weapon in search of his next target. He never did get another.

Though the rifle was less than ideal at such a distance, Maggie had been trained by some of the best shooters in the world. She sent three shots the sniper's way. The first bullet struck true, followed by the second. The third missed, but it didn't matter since the others landed in his head.

A blast came from behind her, but Maggie stayed focused knowing Ashton had her back. She felt him take refills from the belt around her shoulder as she shifted her sights from the gym roof across to the firing range and let loose.

The second sniper went down, and Maggie turned her attention back to the room. "Where's Nina?"

"I don't know," Ashton said, shooting again and taking most of an assassin's head off his shoulders.

"Why are there so many of these bloody bastards?" Viktor hadn't been lying when he boasted about the number of assassins in his employ.

"Grace spotted reinforcements arriving from the rear entrance not long after you. She wanted to ambush them, but we were afraid it would give away your plan."

"We need to find Nina," Maggie said, shooting two new arrivals as they ran in through the side door.

"I don't see her in the mix."

Maggie's face grew slick with blood from the cut on her cheek and drips ran down her neck. It stung, but not as much as the thought of not being the one to take Nina out.

The Unit agents had gotten the better of the Handler's troops, the numbers now in their favor. Still, bodies of her old colleagues lay scattered across Ashton's floor, even more lives for Maggie to fret over once this was all over.

"Come on," Maggie said to Ashton, following her away from the melee. "You check this floor, I'll go downstairs. I told Tami and Gillian to make a run for it, but be on the lookout for them just in case."

"Got it." Ashton knew the house better than anyone, and Maggie watched him leave before taking the stairs.

The fighting had spread down there too, and Maggie did her best to avoid getting caught up in a tussle with anyone. Sweat beaded her forehead, and every part of her ached, but she couldn't stop now. Her final target was so close she could feel it.

Rifle at the ready, Maggie held the pistol grip and kept her finger over the trigger.

An assassin rounded the corner from the kitchen, but she was ready, and fired three bullets into the man, a holy trinity of two in the chest and one through the temple.

The table she, Ash, and Tami sat at the morning after she'd found Leon dead had been knocked over, the chairs broken into pieces with smears of blood over the floor. A shock of red trailed across the marble flooring and Maggie followed it. A foot stuck out from behind the fridge, and she inched closer to inspect.

Heavy panting followed next, and she found a young woman on the floor holding on to a tear across her stomach. Maggie had witnessed enough war wounds to know a lost cause. From the smell of it, the girl's intestines had been cut open. Her sweat-slicked skin had turned deathly pale.

The tactical gear told Maggie the woman belonged to the Unit, but she didn't recognize her face. A new recruit, judging by her age. She couldn't have been more than twenty-one, yet she wouldn't live to see her next birthday.

The girl tried to speak, but only blood escaped her lips and flowed down her face. "Shh," Maggie hushed, reaching for her hand. "Don't try to talk. I'm here with you."

Blood matted the young agent's short blond hair, and she groaned as she tried to move, fear painted across her face. She knew what was happening. Of course she did. If she was anything like Maggie, the girl knew death. Had likely done her fair share of doling it out already.

As though peering into a mirror of her past, Maggie recalled how eager and willing to prove herself she had been at that stage in her life. Lethal and used as a weapon, yet still naive in so many ways. She knew the risks of joining the Unit as much as the girl before her did, but Maggie knew she hadn't believed death would come for her so early. She certainly hadn't, throwing herself into things with reckless abandon, feeling powerful and invincible, like she could take on anything in the world.

Maggie squeezed the woman's hand, unable to do anything but give her this last small comfort as gurgling came from her lungs. Stroking her forehead, Maggie held the girl's gaze while she convulsed, not leaving until her eyes closed forever.

"How touching," grumbled a voice as Maggie was dragged away from the girl's body by the hair. She fumbled for the rifle, but she'd put it down to see to the girl and her fingers grazed over the barrel.

Hair ripped from her scalp as she twisted away from her attacker's grip only to be grabbed by another. The larger of the two, a burly man with veins popping from his neck and muscled arms, punched Maggie in the gut as his partner clung to her. Pain rippled through her body at the sheer forced behind the blow and she would have doubled over had the other man not held her steady.

Laughter echoed in Maggie's ear as the man behind her cackled while she took another blow, this one cracking at least two ribs. She bit back a scream, not giving either of the brutes any satisfaction, and instead stomped hard on the ground with one foot after the other.

The man holding her moved his feet, believing she was trying to crush his toes.

Idiot.

Twin blades protruded from the tips of Maggie's boots, the custom design one of a few pairs she owned with the same handy feature.

The burly man came for her again, aiming for the ribs he'd just broken to inflict even more damage. Maggie leaned her weight back against the other assassin and swung her leg up as high as she could.

"Shit," said the assassin holding her as they both watched the hidden blade catch the brute under his chin. He froze for a moment, but when Maggie's leg dropped, he dropped with it to bleed out on the floor with the dead girl.

Without missing a beat, Maggie stabbed her shoe-knife into the boot of the remaining assassin. His hold of her released as he yelped and she stumbled free, pouncing for the rifle she left by the girl's body. She landed hard on her shoulder, ignoring the agony her newly broken ribs sent shooting through the rest of her body.

The assassin caught on to what she was doing and pulled out a SMG a few seconds too late as Maggie rained down on him with a shower of bullets, not stopping until the magazine ran out and the man collapsed beside his comrade.

Out of breath and wincing at the continual aching from too many wounds, Maggie forced herself to get back up. Her work wasn't over. Not by a long shot.

Water spurted from the kitchen sink and she quickly wiped blood away from her eyes and off her face, drying quickly with Ashton's good dish towels before sneaking out of the kitchen and heading toward the living room.

The tell-tale signs of fighting continued on the floor above, but things had quieted below. Every step Maggie made felt too loud as she continued her search for Nina.

"Maggie, watch out!" called a voice she recognized as Tami's.

She spotted her friend hiding behind the couch and panicked that she was still in the house as an arm wrapped around Maggie's waist and the tip of a knife hovered at her throat.

"You fought well, Ms. Black, but the time comes for us all to die," said the Handler.

Chapter 29

The knife felt cool against her neck. Maggie didn't move a muscle, knowing all it would take was one simple flick of the wrist for the Handler to slit her throat.

A satisfied laugh rumbled in Viktor Fedorov's chest and he pierced her skin with the tip of the blade, just deep enough for a bead of blood to run free. "I had of course hoped my men would take you out back in Moscow, but I must admit, a part of me was glad to learn you survived so *I* could be the one to end your pathetic existence."

His spicy cologne clung to the back of her throat as she kept her breathing steady. Solid muscle held her in a vise grip stronger than Maggie had expected. Tami had ducked back behind the sofa, but the Handler didn't appear to notice her, his focus too pinned on Maggie.

"Your men died screaming," she replied, keeping him talking and hoping to god that Tami made a run for it while she still could.

"As will you. I promised you that day in Café Pushkin that you'd live to regret threatening my family."

Maggie had only needed information from Viktor to help track down one of Bishop's associates. She knew he'd never give it up without good reason and tracking down his wife and daughter had been the most effective way of getting him to spill. "I never would have hurt them. I had ample opportunity to."

That didn't matter, though. For a man like the Handler, the insult damaged not only his ego but threatened his reputation should news of the blackmail leak into the criminal underworld he dwelled in. No one wanted to hire assassins from a man who gave away the names of his clients.

"A weakness of yours, it seems, since you failed to kill Nina's mother and daughter."

Maggie tried to pull Viktor's knife arm away from her, but her attempts failed. He stood a good head and shoulders taller than her and pinned her to him with ease. She had been right to fear the man the first time she met him. While no longer an assassin himself, he had stayed as fit as any of his killers. People like him didn't see their fifties without being hard as nails, and the thick white scars across his hands detailed a lifetime of fighting.

"I don't make a habit of killing innocent people,"

Maggie said, furious at being caught by him. She leaned back, trying to steer him away from the sofa, and forced him to take a few steps to steady himself.

"From what I hear, you do," he said, pressing the knife in a fraction more. "You simply didn't know it at the time. Misguided fool."

"How much is Nina paying you to help her?" Maggie asked, weighing her options. Her special boots were still armed, but as soon as she struck, Fedorov would slice her open. Panic drummed inside her, her heartbeat pounding loud in her ears.

It couldn't end like this. Not until she found Nina and made her pay for what she did.

Viktor leaned closer to her ear, setting the hairs on her neck on end. "Oh, this is free of charge."

Movement flitted in Maggie's periphery, and her heart plummeted as Tami came toward them instead of running away to make her escape.

"Run," Maggie warned. "Get out of here." She made to stab the Handler with her boot blades, desperate to create a distraction, but he saw it coming and avoided her with ease, squeezing her tighter to him.

Tami stood her ground and faced the Handler from twelve short feet away. Maggie's chest rose up and down as unfiltered fear for Tami's life infected her resolve. She eyed the door, motioning for her friend to get out before it was too late.

"Let her go," Tami ordered, aiming the pistol Maggie had given her straight at them.

"What do we have here?" Fedorov asked, his tone mocking and amused.

The gun shook in her untrained grip, but she glared at Viktor with her chin raised. "I said let her go, asshole."

The Handler huffed, forcing Maggie to move as he and Tami circled each other. "Or what?"

"Or I'll shoot you where you stand."

Though she held the weapon with both hands, Tami's grip was all wrong. She'd also left the safety on, a vital detail the Handler would have undoubtably noticed too.

Viktor positioned himself directly behind Maggie, using her as a shield. "I admire your bravery, but Maggie and I have some unfished business we must settle. If you run along now and leave us to it, I won't kill you when I'm done with her."

Tami didn't move. "You won't kill either of us," she spat, that unyielding rage Maggie warned her about igniting behind her dark brown eyes. "Now drop the knife."

While she put on a good show, Tami oozed inexperience. The Handler could slash Maggie's throat and be on her friend in a split second, and he knew it.

Viktor laughed again, milking the moment for his enjoyment like a lion toying with his food. "You're going to have to shoot me, little dove. I'm not letting this bitch go now that I finally have her."

Tami moved back a little, keeping her eyes trained on them. She knocked into the chair behind her and almost stumbled over it. "You think I won't do it?"

"I think if you try, you're going to end up shooting your friend. That would be very unfortunate. I have plans for her before I finally let her die." Viktor whispered in Maggie's ear again. "You're going to beg me to end your life before the night is through. After I kill the girl."

"Tami, please leave," Maggie begged, knowing how this would end if she didn't. Yet she knew Tami's answer before she even spoke, the fierce determination she showed in training evident in the clench of her jaw.

"I'm not going anywhere. Not without you."

Fighting continued upstairs, the commotion indicating that the war wasn't won just yet. No one was coming to save them, and the next person to walk through the living room door could be one of Viktor's assassins. Maggie weighed the odds, knowing Viktor would make good on his promise to murder Tami.

Out of options, Maggie gave Tami a slow, imperceptible nod, the knife nicking her skin further as she did. "Remember what I taught you."

Before Fedorov had time to register what Maggie meant, Tami aimed the gun and fired. It clicked, but no bullet shot out since Tami had neglected to remove the safety.

"Safety," Maggie yelled.

Tami tried again, following Maggie's lessons and aiming the way she'd shown her. Maggie closed her eyes and waited for the pain to slam into her as a thunderous boom echoed through the room.

It never came.

Viktor let out an odd groan and his grip slackened. Maggie shoved herself free of him, careful of the knife, and spun to face him in a fight.

But there was no need. Slack mouthed, Fedorov swayed as Maggie grimaced at his face. Tami's aim hadn't missed. The bullet had torn straight through the Handler's left eye and out the back of his skull.

The Handler was dead by the time he hit the floor.

Tami stood wide-eyed and staring at the gun.

"You did it," Maggie said, crossing the room and wrapping her arms around her. "You killed him."

"I was—I was aiming for his shoulder."

They both turned back to the dead man with a destroyed eye and half the back of his head missing. "Thank god you missed, then," Maggie said, leading Tami out the living room to the front door. "Now hurry up and get out of here."

"But—"

"But nothing," Maggie said, practically shoving Tami

outside and pointing to the collection of Unit vehicles down the driveway. "Did Gillian make it out?"

"We both did, but I ran back," Tami said, looking reluctant to leave without Maggie. "What about you? Aren't you coming with me?"

Maggie took Tami's pistol from her and checked the magazine. "I'm not leaving until Nina is dead."

Chapter 30

Maggie scoured the house in search of Nina. It had been a close one with the Handler, but now he was dead and his partner in crime would soon join him. The fighting had wound down and Maggie passed familiar faces as Unit agents cuffed the remaining living assassins and dragged them away. They may have survived the battle, but they would soon wish they hadn't.

Assassins, especially ones working for the likes of the Handler, were privy to a treasure trove of information that could prove useful to the British government. Once her old agency had squeezed out every bit of information from their new captives, by any means necessary, they'd join their fallen comrades.

"Do you have Nina in custody?" Maggie asked Joseph Hill, a handsome agent who'd joined the Unit a few years before she did. He stopped dragging a blood-ied-up assassin he'd apprehended and dropped him in a squirming heap on the floor.

"I'm not sure. They're still rounding up what's left of the others upstairs."

Maggie returned to Ashton's office. Or at least, what used to be his office.

Pages of destroyed books lay scattered across the blood-soaked carpet, dust, debris, and bodies covering most of the floor. Maggie stepped over the mess to the ruined maple desk where Ashton sat. He'd come out of the fight better than Maggie, though she couldn't tell which of his injuries were from today and which ones were from Russia.

Ashton gestured with open arms to the scene of the massacre. "Welcome to my office, Mags. How can I help you?"

"Did you find Nina?"

"No."

"Did the Unit get her?"

Ashton shrugged and nodded to the door. "Ask her."

Director General Grace Helmsley marched into the room, impeccable in a navy power suit with not a hair out of place, and two bodyguards at her heels.

Tami and Gillian came in behind her and headed straight for them, taking Maggie in their arms. "Thank god you're okay. I was worried sick," Gillian said, tucking back the strands of hair stuck to Maggie's face.

"And you, too," Tami said, moving over to Ashton and barreling into him with a fierce embrace.

Seeing them alive and well, if a little bruised up, settled some of the incessant nerves racking through Maggie. Her friends were safe again, for now.

Ambulances arrived outside and parked in the driveway next to the Unit's fleet of vans, sirens off so as not to draw too much unwanted attention. Maggie hoped they'd brought enough body bags.

"Did you get Nina?" Maggie asked Helmsley, releasing herself from Gillian's fussing.

"No," Grace replied, face dark as storm clouds. "We haven't seen a sign of her since the fighting broke out."

Maggie swore. "You had no one patrolling the grounds or perimeters?"

The director general crossed her arms. "In case you hadn't noticed, my agents were too busy saving your arse from immediate death."

A scream burst from Maggie's throat. She thrashed her arm across the nearest bookshelf and sent hardbacks crashing to the floor around her. A vase had somehow survived the commotion and Maggie sent her boot right through it. Pieces of ceramic crumbled under the force, just like her broken heart.

"By all means, carry on," Ashton said, swirling in his chair. "There's an antique clock on that shelf there. Why don't you put a fist through it."

Gillian gasped as she took in the state of the place. "Oh, Ashton. Your house."

"Och, it's all right. I've been meaning to redecorate anyway."

Grace stomped up to Maggie and slapped her, hard. "Enough."

Maggie froze and glared at her old boss, the shock of being struck stopping her in her tracks more so than any pain it caused. Helmsley's bodyguards stepped forward, anticipating a retaliation, but instead Maggie stopped her raging, shoulders moving up and down as she tried to get her breathing under control.

"We need to find her," she managed.

Grace straightened her suit jacket. "My agents have searched the entire house and grounds. If she was here, they would have found her. I've put out an APW and warned the authorities. I have every available agent working on this. I want her found just as much as you do."

Maggie shook her head. "It's not good enough."

"It's the best I can do," Grace said, knowing the truth of it as much as Maggie. None of those measures would work if Nina had gotten far enough away during the battle.

Blood dripped over Maggie's right eye and she swiped it away. "If she gets away now, she'll come back. It might not be tomorrow, or next week, but she will bide her time and plan her next strike on us like she did before. Each of us has almost died because of her, and I can't stand the thought of losing anyone else. Even you, Grace. I can't and I won't."

Grace knew the danger as much as any of them, having been kidnapped by Ivan Dalca the year before thanks to Nina's attempts at destroying the Unit. She'd also lost far too many agents to Nina and her accomplices' exploits.

"We need to get out there and find her," Maggie said, heading for the door. A car would be best, one of Ashton's fast sports cars to cover more ground.

Gillian stood in her way and blocked the exit. "Look at yourself. You're in no fit state to do much of anything. You need to be checked over by the medics and likely spend an overnight in the hospital."

As if they heard Gillian, Maggie's broken ribs sent shooting pains across her torso. "I'm fine," she lied.

Dr. Park's pain meds were back at Engage, left there as she and the others prepared their plans to try and ambush Nina. Not that it worked. Maggie would kill, literally, for something to take the edge off. If she stopped now, she'd never get back up. The urge to crawl under the blankets of her bed and never get out grew too strong.

But she had no bed to return to. The bed she shared with Leon still had his blood over it. Still lay in the apartment she could never return to again.

Maggie held up her hands. "Okay, okay. I'm listening. I need to use the bathroom and clean up a little."

She made to leave, but Gillian didn't budge. "I'll come with you."

"I can manage on my own, thanks."

"I know, but please humor me. I want to see to it that you're taken care of."

Maggie held her temper, knowing all of their eyes were on her. "Fine."

"You're going to need stitches," Gillian said, examining the cut at the side of Maggie's face. "The gash on your neck might be able to go without."

More scars.

Leon used to trace hers with his fingers when they made love, both of them covered in mementos from their dangerous exploits, filled with narrow misses and close calls.

She caught a glimpse of herself in the mirror and got a fright. Hollow cheeks, drawn face, and dark bags under her eyes. And all of that was before the cuts, swelling, and bruises. Averting her gaze, she focused on cleaning her open wounds, making sure to remove any dirt.

"I need a shower," she said with a grimace. Her clothes stuck to her, covered with blood and dried sweat.

Gillian nodded and helped her peel free from her clothes. Tears pricked at Gillian's eyes as she gasped at

Maggie's naked frame. Her pale skin resembled a muddy camouflage of red, purple, and dull yellow.

"It's not as bad as it looks," she said, having to rely on her friend to undo her boots and remove her socks. Bending over with her broken ribs sent dark spots across her vision and made her head spin.

The water hissed to life, and Gillian checked the temperature before allowing Maggie in.

"I've got it from here." Maggie stepped under the hot water and closed the glass door, clamping her jaw to stop from whimpering as the heat stung her abrasions.

Gillian looked ready to argue.

"I need a few moments on my own," she pleaded, not needing to lie.

"I'll be right outside. Call if you need me."

"Thanks, Gill," Maggie said, feeling bad for being short-tempered. "I love you."

"I love you, too. Take all the time you need."

Maggie forced the tears back as Gillian left, sick of crying. Sick of feeling empty yet simultaneously flooded with too much emotion. It exhausted her more than the physical exertion she'd put her body through the last few days. Hurt more than any stab wound, blow to the head, gun shot, or broken bone, all of which she'd sustained in her failed attempts at stopping Nina.

Focusing on the task of cleaning herself, Maggie scrubbed, lathered, and washed the suds from her hair and body. Her lips chattered as she stepped out and wrapped a soft towel around herself, keeping the water running so Gillian didn't hear.

Collecting the phone from her jeans pocket took longer than she cared to admit, but she finally sat herself down on the closed toilet and turned it on.

The screen had cracked at some point, from one of the many falls she'd taken, but it still worked. Searching for the fake bingo app, Maggie opened the encrypted two-way chat and began to type.

There were many things she wished to say to her old friend, but none of it mattered. She got straight to the point instead.

ENOUGH BACK AND FORTH. WE END THIS. JUST THE TWO OF US. NO ONE ELSE.

A few agonizing minutes passed, and Maggie had almost given up when a response arrived.

AGREED. HOW DO YOU WANT TO DO THIS?

A FAIR FIGHT, Maggie sent back. NO WEAPONS. NO BACKUP.

WHERE AND WHEN?

Maggie pondered the most strategic place, not trusting Nina for one second to follow the rules. THE SPOT WE USED TO GO JOGGING. MIDNIGHT TONIGHT.

SEE YOU THEN.

YOU BETTER.

Maggie hit send then turned off the phone. She had a lot to prepare for their final meeting, but first she really did need to see a medic.

Chapter 31

London, Great Britain

Maggie pulled up in Ashton's sleek black Jaguar and parked on Queen's Road ten minutes before midnight. Richmond Park, one of London's busiest spots for locals to escape the busy streets and hustle and bustle of city life, had emptied as night fell.

Only a few remained. Dog walkers getting off a backshift at work. Lovers meeting up for secret trysts. Nothing out of the ordinary for a London park. A fight to the death, however, was another matter.

And it would be to the death. Only one of them

would walk away, and Maggie planned to fight tooth and nail to make sure it was her.

Gillian had been right about needing a night in hospital. The medics on site at Ashton's wanted to take Maggie there and then, but she refused, allowing them to patch her up and meet with the Unit's doctor Sabina Rajinder instead, who confirmed what she already knew.

Her ribs were indeed broken, though thankfully they didn't suspect any internal bleeding. According to Dr. Rajinder, Dr. Park had done a good job attending to her first stab wound. Though it hadn't had much time to heal, nor had Maggie taken his advice to rest, Sabina reconfirmed that no internal organs had been damaged from the attack. She stitched up the cut on the side of Maggie's head and prescribed antibiotics to avoid infection.

Maggie requested a shot of morphine to tackle the pain. Just enough to calm it down to a manageable level while still being able to keep her wits about her. She'd need them.

Ashton had cleaners come in and do what they could in the aftermath, though the place still resembled a war zone by the time Maggie said goodnight to her friends, claiming an early night. Given everything she'd been through, they bought it without question, and Maggie began her preparations.

Her room had gone untouched in the fighting, and her spare clothes and items Ashton had brought from her apartment remained right where she left them. Maggie refused to give Nina the satisfaction of seeing the full extent of her injuries, and spent some time applying thick layers of makeup to conceal what she could.

A bulletproof vest wouldn't have been a bad idea to wear, but Maggie wanted to avoid anything getting in the way of her agility. Nina fought fast. Instead, she put on all-black gym clothes, the same ones she wore when out enjoying some parkour with the boys, and tied her hair out of the way into a tight bun.

She'd spotted an abandoned Desert Eagle lying on the floor on her way to her room, designed in ostentatious titanium gold that must have belonged to one of the Handler's assassins. Maggie scooped up the semi-automatic pistol before anyone noticed, thankful to discover a full magazine.

They had agreed not to use weapons, but Maggie knew not to take Nina's word on anything, and any notion of fighting fair had gone out the window after she killed Leon.

Slipping out had been easy. Gillian had gone home to her family, while Tami and Ashton had retired to their own rooms, each as exhausted as Maggie and falling into a deep slumber. Certain they were both sleeping, Maggie ventured downstairs and into Ashton's garage, making sure to select one of his quieter cars.

Now that she had arrived at their meeting spot, it occurred to her she should have left some kind of note for them, just in case. Too late now.

Maggie got out of the car and tucked the gun into her waistband behind her back. No streetlights lined the road and darkness enclosed around her as soon as she locked the car. She waited until her eyes adjusted, keeping watch for any sign of Nina.

In an ideal world, Maggie would have arrived at the park hours before to stake out the area in case Nina planned any more of her tricks. Doing so would have given Ashton and Tami time to notice she was gone, and they could have tracked her down before midnight. This way meant that even if they did discover her bed empty and tracked Ashton's car, they'd be too late to stop her thanks to the ninety-minute drive.

Confident of her surroundings after a few minutes, Maggie left the road and ventured further into the park. Trees towered over her like ancient spectators, eagerly awaiting the big fight. A light wind wafted through the leaves on their full branches and brought a pleasant breeze to the humid air. It would be a hot day tomorrow, and Maggie hoped she lived to see it.

Branches snapped under her shoes, each echoing through the silent night with only the coos of owls to keep her company. She avoided traversing the worn pathways, wishing to stay out of sight for as long as possible.

Richmond Park had been a familiar haunt of Maggie and Nina's. They'd meet up there on their days off to go for a jog, using the exercise as an excuse to catch up and share some office gossip, detailing their latest missions and whatever personal drama they were going through. They'd been real friends once, and no matter how much Maggie thought on it, she couldn't pinpoint the moment where all that changed.

None of it mattered now.

Their "spot" that Maggie had referred to was Pen Ponds. After their run, they'd grab a coffee and something sweet from the permanent food-truck nearby and sit by the stretch of water while they ate. Secluded now, and well out of the way of any bystanders, it made for the perfect meeting place.

The moon reflected off the water's surface, rippling from the wind. Tufts of wild grass sprouted across the surrounding land, creating an uneven terrain far from ideal for what was about to go down.

Maggie walked over it with careful footing until she arrived at a patch of hard-packed sand that ran along the banks of the pond.

"I didn't think you'd come."

Maggie spun on her heel toward the voice as Nina stepped into view from behind a thicket of bushes. Like Maggie, she wore all black and had had similar thoughts about her hair, pinning it back from her face.

"I wouldn't miss it," Maggie said. The tension grew thick in the air as they sized each other up. "Show me your weapon."

"Show me yours," Nina retorted, stepping onto the

sandy banks, not even trying to deny she had something on her.

"I don't want a shoot-out. I want to kill you with my bare hands." Maggie slowly reached around for her gun and held it in the air. Nina did the same.

"The feeling's mutual. Throw yours in the lake with me."

Maggie counted down from three, and to her surprise, Nina carried through and tossed her gun into the pond along with Maggie's Desert Eagle. They plopped into the water and sank to the murky depths, out of reach and of no use to either of them.

"We could have done this in the first place," Maggie said, holding her position twenty feet away. "I would have come."

After what Nina had pulled with Ivan Dalca, Maggie knew she couldn't be allowed to live. Her disregard for the second chance Maggie had offered her made that crystal clear, her need for retribution overpowering anything else. Maggie would have come, and no one else had to die.

Nina sneered. "I wanted to watch you suffer first."

"I see why you came back instead of staying hidden and taking care of Cara. You're not capable of raising a child. All you would do is raise her to be a monster like you."

Fiona would see to it that her granddaughter grew up in a normal, healthy environment, filled with love, in a way Nina could never provide. Maggie took no pleasure in making a child an orphan, having been one herself, but it had to be done.

Nina sighed, too far away for Maggie to see if her words stung the way she intended. "Are you done talking?"

Making use of the pent-up emotions warring within her, Maggie didn't say another word and charged at her enemy. Nina followed suit, and the ex-agents collided in the middle of the deserted park with murderous intent.

Both women were trained in mixed martial arts and had always been an equal match. Yet the high stakes and personal vendetta had made each of them reckless and wild.

Nina came at her with a flying kick, springing on her heels as Maggie drew nearer. She saw it coming and grabbed Nina in mid-air, tossing her to the sand and landing a boot square in her chest.

Her opponent fell back, but Nina used the momentum and rolled onto her feet. She reached for her ankle and Maggie caught the glint of metal reflecting off the moonlight.

So much for fighting fair.

Nina closed the gap between them and came at her with the knife. Maggie dodged the first attack, knowing how Nina liked to lace the edges of her blades with poison.

A second attempt caught Maggie across the stomach,

ripping her shirt as she pivoted too late and barely missed her skin. She couldn't risk a third and lashed out with a roundhouse kick. It connected, hitting Nina's wrist, and the blade flew from her hands into the pond beside them.

Nina made to retrieve it, but Maggie smacked her with a right hook and sent a flurry of blows her way. They all connected, Maggie unrelenting in her advance and putting everything she had into each hit.

A few punches weren't enough to stop someone like Nina, and she returned the favor, clipping Maggie square in the face and bursting her nose. A roundhouse came next, right in her ribs.

Waves of agony coursed through her and Maggie let out an involuntary scream into the night and fell to her knees.

Nina's eyes lit at the display, more cunning than a city fox. "Looks like you've broken a few of your ribs."

On her again before Maggie could get up, Nina lashed out with another kick, followed by a series of jabs to her weak spot. Nausea overcame Maggie as she struggled not to fall, knowing she might not ever get up again.

Instead, she launched herself at Nina and clumsily clung to her legs. Though not the most skillful takedown attempt, Maggie put all of her weight behind it, and Nina fell to meet her on the damp sand.

They rolled around in it, grains sticking to everything they touched as both women fought for control. Maggie dug an elbow into Nina's gut and wrapped her legs around her waist, forcing herself on top of her.

Gaining the upper hand, Maggie smelled victory and punched Nina in the jaw so hard she felt teeth unroot.

Nina wriggled under her, reaching into her pocket instead of blocking the attacks, until something wet sprayed into Maggie's face.

As soon as it landed, she knew what it was. Mace.

Maggie's eye stung like crazy but she knew better than to rub at them.

"You conniving, cheating bitch."

Swinging blind, Maggie hit Nina again, but her adversary headbutted her in return. It sent Maggie reeling back as the impact made her mind swim in confusion.

She tried to scramble to her feet, but Nina barged into her and pinned her arms into the sand. Maggie blinked back tears from the Mace, Nina appearing on top of her like a distorted ghost from her messed-up vision.

Fighting to get free, Nina slapped her with a back-hand and opened up the newly stitched cut at the side of her head. Sand grated into Maggie's back, the grains everywhere now. She dug her heels into it, trying to push herself up, but the softness of it sent her feet sliding.

Nina's eyes landed on something to the left, and Maggie turned to follow her line of sight. Through leaking eyes, she watched helplessly as Nina picked up a large rock.

"I've got you now," she said in a manic shrill.

Maggie wailed as Nina bludgeoned her in the head, adrenaline pumping through her veins as imminent death approached. She couldn't withstand another one, already weak and running on nothing but fumes.

Leon flashed in her mind as Nina pulled back for another blow. Maggie could almost hear him telling her to get up. To fight.

Nina came down on her again, and Maggie screamed. She put every last bit of energy she had left into twisting underneath her enemy, moving just enough for the rock to sink into the sand where her head had laid a split second before.

Desperate to survive, Maggie dug a thumb into Nina's eye.

It was Nina's turn to scream, and she pulled away on instinct, dropping the rock and reaching for her eye.

Maggie took the opportunity. She picked up the rock from the sand and clubbed Nina across the head with it. Nina swayed, and Maggie bashed her again so hard she was able to pin her opponent just like she had done to her.

Without hesitation, Maggie struck her, again and again until Nina stopped fighting to get her off of her.

Maggie stopped, the rock dripping red, and blinked through watering eyes at Nina's mess of a face.

Nina coughed weakly; her teeth coated with blood as she wheezed short, shallow breaths.

"You're right, you know," she said, staring up into the night sky. "I would have been a terrible mother."

Shaking hands pulled something from the pocket of her black hoodie but the item fell through her fingers. A photo of little Cara fluttered to the sand, taken not long after she was born from the size of her.

Maggie took the photo and placed it in Nina's hand. She brought the photo of her daughter to her lips and then held it to her heart, ready for what was to come next.

"Goodbye, Nina" Maggie said, before picking up the rock again and giving her old friend one final, killing blow to the head.

Chapter 32

23 June
Essex, Great Britain

Cemeteries always felt cold to Maggie, even in the middle of summer.

It had only been two days since that night in Richmond Park, but the time had come to say her final goodbyes to the love of her life.

The last week had been a whirlwind of one disaster after another, and she'd barely had time for anything to really sink in. Now, seeing Ashton and the men in Leon's family carry his coffin from the back of the hearse hit her like a ton of bricks.

Her legs shook, and she had to hold on to Tami to

keep herself steady. Grace stood to her right, as stoic and hard-faced as the bodyguards behind her. Even so, Maggie caught her dabbing at her eyes before putting on her sunglasses.

Gillian stood at the other side of the hole in the ground, her husband and kids beside her as she openly wept. Unit agents mixed in with the crowd, all gathered there to pay respects to their fallen chief and friend. A few had stopped to express their condolences to Maggie, and she nodded along and said the right things, numb to all of it.

The service had been nice; what little Maggie heard of it. She'd gone through most of it in a trance, unable to focus on the words of the minister. Most of the day had gone by like that, from waking up and having Tami help her get dressed, the long drive from Ashton's house to the church, then on to Epping Cemetery.

Sade stood by the minister, huddled with her sisters while Idris helped with the coffin. He'd held up remarkably well to be able to do that, and Maggie admired him more than ever for the strength it took. They'd both done so well, with Sade's words in the church bringing everyone at the service to tears.

Leon had been so loved by many. Had touched so many lives.

Maggie averted her eyes from Leon's parents. She'd been avoiding them, waiting until his aunts had taken up the seats next to them in the church before finding a pew.

They'd had to organize the funeral last minute thanks to being stuck away somewhere under Unit protection. They'd only gotten back yesterday, Grace not wanting to risk letting them return home until she was certain it was safe for them to do so.

Maggie knew she should have stopped by last night, or met with them earlier that morning, but she couldn't think what to say to them. Didn't want to know what they thought of her now that they knew the truth.

A lump caught in Maggie's throat as the coffin reached the gathering crowd. They parted to make way and she swayed, gripping onto Tami's hand as they lowered Leon into the ground. Nausea swept through her and she felt the blood drain from her face.

One by one, people dropped white roses and dirt into the six-foot hole before walking away to the rows of parked cars. Tami left Maggie with Gillian to pay her own respects. She knew better than to hug or fuss over her right now. Maggie couldn't bear it.

As the crowd thinned, it became impossible to avoid Leon's parents. They stood at the foot of their son's grave, embracing each other in their sorrow. Maggie walked over to them on hesitant feet.

"Sade, Idris," she said, crying already. "I don't know what to say."

"Grace explained everything to us," Idris said, checking over his shoulder as if to make sure no one heard them. "I'd be lying if I said we weren't in shock about it all. It's one thing to have to bury your son so young, but to know that he was murdered..."

"Your son was a hero," Maggie told them. "The best of us all."

The sun shone down on them, its brightness almost an insult to their reason for standing between the rows and rows of headstones.

"From what Grace tells us, you're quite the hero yourself," Idris said, still sounding overwhelmed at the idea of his son and his girlfriend being secret agents for the British government. It was a far cry from the office manager they thought Leon had been.

"I'm no hero," Maggie said, tucking a strand of hair behind her ear, conscious of the state of her face. Makeup could only cover so much, and she'd heard Ashton tell someone at the church that she'd been in the car crash that had taken Leon, making the most of the Unit's cover story for his death.

Sade took her hand, both of them trembling with the stress of the day. "They told us you found the woman who did it to him. That she's dead now, too."

"She is," Maggie said, though she took no joy in the fact. The entire mess had caused so much needless death, Bishop's actions resulted in a catastrophic domino effect that many would never recover from.

"God forgive me, but I'm glad," Sade said. Her anger vanished as soon as it appeared, and Maggie bowed her head, unable to look them in the face.

JACK MCSPORRAN

"I understand if you don't want to speak to me after this."

Sade stepped forward and cupped Maggie's face, gently raising her head until she met her gaze. "None of this was your fault, Maggie. Leon wouldn't want you blaming yourself for the actions of others."

Maggie closed her eyes. "I don't know what I'm going to do without him."

Arms wrapped around her, and Sade's flowery perfume filled her senses. "You're coming round to our place for Sunday lunch, I know that much. We still love you, no matter what. You hear me?"

Maggie could only nod, unable to speak.

Idris came and hugged her, too, resembling Leon so much it hurt. "I'll save you a seat at the gathering. I want you sitting with us at the family table."

They had arranged a send-off for Leon at a local bar and restaurant for those who wanted to attend after the funeral proceedings, as a way for those who loved him to celebrate of his life.

Maggie took a deep breath and gathered herself. "I'll be there. I just need a few more minutes."

They left with the others and Maggie stood alone by Leon's grave. Ashton and Tami waited for her by the car, giving her space. She didn't know how long she stood there, talking to him. The words just came, like it was a normal morning back at the flat, chatting before Leon went off to work.

288

Those were some of her favorite memories of him. The simple ones. Of talking over breakfast and laughing during their strolls around the city. Of nights spent on the couch cuddling into each other and watching old movies. Just having him around her and being able to fall asleep in his arms had been a dream, and she would never forget the little things for as long as she lived.

Leon had brought light into her life at a time she never thought it was possible, and ever since he had loved her like she'd never been loved by another person in the world. He was her soulmate, in every sense of the word, and though their time together had been shorter than she imagined, Maggie thought herself lucky to have known him in ways no one else did.

No matter where she went, or what lay in store for her in the future, she'd carry him with her, and he'd never be forgotten.

Maggie let go of the white rose she held, and it fell on top of the coffin with the others. "Goodbye, Leon. I love you, always."

Chapter 33

30 June
West Sussex, Great Britain

Maggie groaned as the curtains opened and light spilled into the stuffy bedroom.

"Come on, sleepy head," Ashton said, chirpier than necessary. "Time to get shifted."

Maggie took her pillow and covered her face from the brightness assaulting her. "What time is it?"

"Three in the afternoon," Tami said, coming in with Willow in her arms. The feline jumped free when she spotted Maggie and landed next to her on the bed. She rubbed against her and meowed in her ear, like a co-conspirator trying to wake her up. Little traitor.

"Just another hour," Maggie said, pulling the sheets over her shoulder and turning around with her back to them.

"You've been like this for seven days now, love," came Gillian's voice, her kitten heels too loud as they click-clacked on the wooden floors. "It's time to face the world."

Maggie didn't move, had barely moved at all since she returned from Leon's funeral. "I've had enough of the world."

Wheels rolled across the floor, and Maggie sat up in defeat, pinching the bridge of her nose. Her hair sat in a nest on her head, and she couldn't remember the last time she'd showered. She didn't see the point in it these days.

Ashton entered the room again, pulling three large suitcases with him.

"What's all this?"

"Your things from the apartment," he said, laying the cases on their backs and zipping them open. "There're plenty of boxes downstairs I need your help with, too."

"We can do it tomorrow," Maggie said, sinking back into her mattress as he popped out into the hallway again.

Willow licked at her face, and she felt the bed shift as Gillian and Tami sat down next to her.

"You know what he's like," Tami said, tapping away on her phone. "Best just to humor him."

"Agreed," Gillian said, getting up and standing over Maggie with her hands on her hips. "Now you go and get a shower, and I'll bring you up a nice cuppa and something to eat."

"But—"

"Chop, chop, Mags," Ashton said, arriving with two more suitcases this time. "You can't sort all your things out on an empty stomach."

"Am I moving in?" she asked. They hadn't discussed it. To be honest, she hadn't thought about living arrangements at all, too lost in her own depression and grief. All she wanted to do was sleep and forget about everything.

"We've all agreed it's for the best," Ashton said, slowing down for a minute to join them on the bed. "You can stay here as long as you want."

Maggie sat up, her muscles stiff from hardly moving for a week. Still, it had given her injured body time to rest. Even her ribs had begun to feel better. "Thanks, Ash. Thank you all for putting up with me."

"Don't be silly," Gillian said. "We're a team."

Ashton cleared his throat. "About that. We've been talking, and we want you to know that we don't need to carry on with Engage if you don't want to."

"No," Maggie said instantly, sitting up straighter. "No, we carry on as planned."

"Don't feel pressured if it's too much for you," Tami began, but Maggie had her mind made up.

She didn't know what her life would be like now that so much had changed. Didn't want to think much about it, either. Truth was, she found it hard enough to get through the day, never mind thinking further ahead. Yet, no matter what she was going through, Maggie was adamant that Engage remain.

"If Leon was here, he'd still be working at the Unit. He'd carry on fighting. And so will I. We have the ability to really make a difference, all four of us. I'm still in, if you guys are."

Nina and Viktor Fedorov were dead, but there were still plenty more like them out there in the world, abusing their power against those helpless to do anything.

Ashton and Tami nodded in agreement, while Gillian let out a little cheer. "Oh, I'm so glad I don't need to throw away my nametag."

Maggie laughed for the first time in a while. It wasn't much, and it felt wrong for so many reasons to find joy in things, but it was a start. She had a long road ahead of her, but with friends like those around her, she could face anything.

She threw the covers back and got out of bed. "All right, let me get ready."

M oving her worldly possessions took longer than she had expected. It was almost midnight, and Maggie, Ashton, and Tami sat in the newly-decorated living room, going over a mountain of paperwork, sorting through bills, letting agreements, insurance policies, and a whole load of junk mail in between.

Gillian had gone home for the evening, and they'd arranged themselves next to the roaring fireplace to enjoy a drink while they worked. "Do you think the landlord will be okay with me breaking the lease?" Maggie asked.

Ashton poured them all another whisky. "I spoke to him yesterday. He's fine with it."

It didn't sound like the shady London landlord she knew, but she chose not to ask any questions about how Ash had managed to make the old tyrant agree to the matter.

"This one looks important," Tami said, passing over a stuffed envelope.

"What is it?" Ashton said, as Maggie's mood changed.

"It's from Bishop's lawyer. The one who settled his estate. I told Leon to throw it out, but he must have kept it." Maggie got up from the couch and walked toward the fireplace, the wood crackling amid the flames.

"Don't you want to see what's inside?" Tami asked. She'd kindly spent the last hour emailing those on Maggie's list of direct debits whose services she no longer needed. Internet, utilities, contents insurance, council tax. At least Maggie stood to save some money while she got her life back together.

Ashton sat back and swirled his drink. "He could have left you something."

"I don't want anything from him," Maggie said,

echoing what she'd told Leon when the package first arrived.

Tami looked thoughtful for a moment. "Perhaps whatever is in there could bring you closure. Everything that happened started because of him."

Maggie paused at that. Leon had said the same thing.

"Whatever it is, it was important enough for him to arrange for it to get to you if he died," Ashton added. "I think you should open it."

Maggie tossed it across the room to him and sat back down. "Fine, if you care so much, you read the bloody thing."

Ashton put down his drink and pulled out the contents of the stuffed envelope.

His brow furrowed as he read over the first letter. He moved on to a collection of papers that were enclosed in a manila envelope resembling the kind used by the Unit. Ashton flicked through the file, slowly at first, picking up speed as his eyes darted across the pages.

Tami sat forward as they waited for him to say something, sharing a worried look with Maggie.

"What?" Maggie asked, heart racing.

Ashton peered up from the pages and stared at her in a way he never had before.

"You're scaring me, Ash. What is it?"

Ashton ran a hand over his face and shook his head in disbelief.

"It's your mum, Mags. She's still alive."

NEVER MISS A RELEASE!

Thank you so much for reading Payback. I hope you enjoyed it!

I have so much more coming your way. Never miss a release by joining my free VIP club. You'll receive all the latest updates on my upcoming books as well as gain access to exclusive content and giveaways!

To sign up, simply visit: https://jackmcsporran.com/download-free-books/

Thank you for reading PAYBACK! If you enjoyed the book, I would greatly appreciate it if you could consider adding a review on your bookstore of choice.

Reviews make a huge difference to the success or failure of a book, especially for writers like myself. The more reviews a book has, the more people are likely to take a shot on picking it up. The review need only be a line or two, and it really would make the world of difference for me if you could spare the three minutes it takes to leave one.

With all my thanks,

Jack McSporran